FLOODED
FLOODED
FLOODED
FLOODED
FLOODED
FLOODED

REQUIEM FOR JOHNSTOWN

FL**OODED**

JOHNSTOWN

A NOVEL IN VERSE BY

ANN E. BURG

SCHOLASTIC PRESS / NEW YORK

In the beginning,
before villages and towns,
my waters were pure
as the melted
mountain snow.
Protected by slopes
verdant
with spruce and hemlock,
surrounded by fields
dotted
with wild berries
and dew-kissed violets,
I blissfully
babbled
and danced.
Silvery pickerel,
bass and trout
sparkled
in the sunlight
and, when storms
raged,
found shelter
within and around
my sunken
logs and rocks.

Earliest inhabitants
respected
the beneficence
of my waters,
and gratefully
offered prayers
for the gifts
I shared.

But the trees
through
which
I happily
rambled
slowly
disappeared.
Townspeople
buried
their waste
on my
narrowing
banks,
and fouled
my water
with night soil
and slag.
The open
fields—
the wild
berries
and
purple
flowers,
the fragrant
hedgerow
and
colorful
underwood—

were unearthed,
the rich,
fertile
soil
carted
away
and
my
natural
river
depths
and
borders
reshaped
and
rebuilt
to
suit
the
ever-
changing
needs
of
man.

PART

O N E

JOE DIXON

My brothers have been tromping
around the house for days
pretending to be Union soldiers.

I don't blame them
for being excited—
Decoration Day
isn't until next Thursday,
but already the town's dressed
in red, white and blue bunting.

Everyone's in a holiday mood—
nodding, smiling,
happy to drop three cents
to read the news of the day.
Good for business!

But with every nod,
smile and thank-you
my heart thumps
like a field drum—

Pa still doesn't know
I bought this newsstand.
He thinks I'm working
at the company store.

You've got to tell him,
Maggie says,

and I want to.
I'm just waiting
for the perfect moment—
a calm, quiet moment.

In our house
that won't happen
in a crow's age.

≋

It's not just the newsstand
making my heart thump.

There's something else.

Something burning
a hole in my pocket.

You made it weeks ago,
my friend Ed says.
Just give it to her.

But I can't. Not yet.
That's got to be
a perfect moment too.

No little brothers pestering.
No well-meaning friends.

Just me, Maggie
and a ring made
of two willow twigs
twisted together—

a promise
of my undying love.
≋

When Maggie's pa died,
my ma cared for her
while her ma cleaned houses.

We played together
morning till night.

Maggie's shimmery blue eyes
look like they're made
of sky-water—
sparkling and wide open,
endless as the sky
above Lake Conemaugh
and even more beautiful.

Someday
I want to give Maggie
a deep-red ruby
set in a circle of gold
like the glittering ring
I saw at Larkin's.

Someone like Maggie
deserves the best.

My newsstand is only
the first step.
I got my heart set

on being a millionaire businessman
like my hero, Andrew Carnegie.

Then I'll be able to afford
a proper engagement ring!

≋

Papers say when Andrew Carnegie
got married, he gave his wife
twenty thousand dollars a year for life—
twenty thousand dollars!

Most folks in Johnstown
won't ever make
twenty thousand dollars—
not in their whole life,
not in twenty lives.

But I will!
If Carnegie can do it,
I can too.
Andrew Carnegie and me
have a lot in common.

My family came from England
and his from Scotland,
but both our families
were immigrants
looking for a better life.

Carnegie was just about
the age I am
when he arrived here
and got a job
as a bobbin boy
in a cotton factory.

A bobbin boy!
Now he's the wealthiest man
in the world.

Everybody's got to start
somewhere!

≋

GERTRUDE QUINN

For the zillionth time,
Miss Wells has us
practicing our song
for Decoration Day.
I can't wait!
It's only six days away!

Papa will wear
his blue soldier uniform
and march in a grand parade
and all the schoolchildren
will meet at the cemetery
so ladies can give us flowers
to put on the graves
of the buried soldiers.

My brother Vincent,
my sisters Helen and Rosemary,
Grandmother, Grandfather,
Uncle Louis, Uncle Andrew,
Aunt Barbara, and Aunt Abbie
will all be there—
Aunt Abbie lives in Kansas
but she's staying with us
to help care for Baby Marie
while Mama is away.
Poor Mama! She's visiting

Uncle Edward in Scottsdale
and will miss all the excitement!

Already, Helen and Rosemary
draped
red, white and blue bunting
across our front porch,
and Vincent helped me
decorate Daisy's barn
and the large wire hutch
where he keeps his pet ducks.

He even made
Helen and Rosemary share
the leftover bunting
so I could decorate
my playroom
way up on the third—

Gertrude! Miss Wells's voice
splashes like ice-cold water.
Stop daydreaming and sing!

The pure, the bright, the beautiful,
I holler, *these things can never die!*
≋

Vincent says Papa's store
has been busy selling bunting
and small cloth flags on a stick.

I love Papa's store!
It has everything—
hats and coats,
collars and shoes,
buttons and boxes,
feathers and fancy lace.

There are knives and glasses
that I mustn't touch,
but Papa keeps these
out of reach.

*Nothing's beyond
our Gertie's reach!*
Vincent laughs.

Best of all are spools
of thread, bolts of fabric
and rolls of ribbon.
And best, best, BEST of all
are the pins and spangles
left sparkling on the floor.

Vincent sweeps twice a day,
but I always find
small treasures
twinkling in the corners.

Papa lets me keep
whatever I find
and doesn't even scold Vincent
for being careless.
He just shakes his head
and smiles—
Can't sell a dusty button.

I promise to sweep more carefully, Pa,
Vincent says, and winks at me.
But I just don't have Gertie's eagle eyes.
≋

Whenever I go to Papa's store,
people I don't even know
smile and pat me on the head.
My goodness, how you've grown!
they tell me.
What a lovely child!
they tell my father.

Who's she? I ask Papa
a hundred times a day.
Who's he?

Papa smiles.
That's Mrs. Baumer,
the postmaster's wife—

Mrs. Blough,
the widow on Waters Street—
Mama took you to visit her
when you were just a baby.

Miss Lavelle,
a dressmaker—

Mrs. Jenkins—
she doesn't live
in Johnstown anymore,
but she visits often.

That's Mr. Dilbert,
who papered your playroom—

Mr. Larkin,
the jeweler—
you've met him before.

That's Mr. Little—
he's the one who brings me
the wooden bowls I sell.
He has a little girl
the same age as you.

Papa should be president.
He knows everyone in Johnstown!
≋

DANIEL FAGAN

Less than a week
until Decoration Day—
then just
one more month
cooped up inside
a sweltering schoolroom,
shackled
to a worn-out desk.

I've got the whole summer
planned—
I'll get up with the sun
and be out of the house
before Ma snares me
with endless chores.

I'll be out of town,
by the bank of the river,
before the fire of the mill
mixes with the heat of the day
and the suffocating stink
of burning steel.

This is the summer
I break free.

Helping care for babies
is women's work.

Monica can entertain Clara
and help feed Tommy.
There's a whole beautiful
world out there.

Even Pa says
it's a boy's nature
and right to explore it.
≋

Today's Friday, so after school,
me, Willy and George
are gonna hike what Willy dubbed
King's Mountain.

We won't make it to the top
where the fancy club is—
takes half a day to hike there—

but we'll see how far we can get
before Willy's old pocket watch
says it's time to head home.

Think I'll bring a bucket
to collect branches for whittling.
≋

Back in late March,
when winter's chill
kept the bloodroot
curled
inside its leaves,
I stumbled on a bummer
coiled up and sleeping
beside the stone leg
of the railroad bridge.
He sat up when he heard me
and began to sing.

A plunge and a splash
and our task was over.

He pulled a small knife
from his pocket
and grabbed the peeled
branch beside him.

The billows rolled
as they rolled before.

I watched as white curls of wood
fell from his fingers
and a wooden bird formed
in his hands.

Can you teach me that?
I asked.

The bummer nodded
and I sat down beside him.
He gave me his knife
and showed me
how to hold it.

Hurt my hand
to grip so tight
but the bummer said
each slash would make
my muscles stronger.

Just don't slice your fingers,
he said.

He held up a dirty,
mangled thumb
and smiled,

his teeth black

as the clouds above Johnstown.

≋

Since then, I sneak back
to the bridge whenever I can
to learn more and hear stories.

Sometimes the bummer
sings songs I've never heard
and sometimes he tells stories.

A few weeks ago,
he told me that
before the mills were built,
the air in Johnstown
was sweet as wild columbine,
as fresh as mountain mint.

Quiet too, he said.
At night you could hear
the wail of the whip-poor-will
and coo of the mourning dove.
You could see shapes
in the stars and make yourself
a wish on the brightest one.

It is hard to imagine.

Even if I didn't always hear
the wheezing whistle of steam
or the constant clank of steel,

even if I didn't always choke
on the foul smell
from the factories,

when I look down
from the craggy spur
of King's Mountain,
all I see
is an inky black veil—

the thick black clouds
of Johnstown
that stole away our stars.

≋

Last Saturday, Ma and me
saw the bummer on our way back
from Mr. Musante's fruit stand.

He was just shuffling
toward us,
holes in his shoes,
holes in his jacket,
holes in the hat
flopped on his head.

*Stay away from that
sorry-looking man,*
Ma said when she saw him.
Disgraceful how some men live.

The bummer tipped his hat
when he saw me
but I turned away.

Pa says bummers are just people
down on their luck.
Just people hoping for a little kindness.

I've been looking for the bummer
ever since.
I'm sorry I turned away, I'll say
and he'll nod and smile.

Pa's been letting me use
his pocketknife.
If I get good enough,
I'm going to whittle
Christmas gifts for everyone—

a flute for Pa,
a new mixing spoon for Ma,
blocks for Clara and Tommy,
a fancy comb for Monica
if she ever stops wakin' the snakes
with her tales and tattles,

and a little star
for the bummer to keep
in his pocket.
≋

WILLIAM JAMES

Miss Dowling's words
spin in my mind
like a whirligig
on a windy day.

After school,
she held in her hand
a red, cloth-covered book
decorated with gold swirls.
I think it would be wonderful
if you could write a poem
to share on Decoration Day.

My breath caught in my chest.

Next Thursday
all the businesses close,
and Pa will wear
his Union uniform
and march
in a grand parade
through town
to the cemetery.
Ma will join the ladies and children
placing flowers on the graves
of dead soldiers.
Burgess Horrell, Mr. Elder
and other important people

will make speeches,
and students will sing
or recite poems.

I—I don't know if I can,
I stammered.

You've been collecting words
for a long time, Willy—
but what a writer needs most
is an open heart,
a heart that sees
what the eye doesn't.

Miss Dowling smiled
and handed me
the book she was holding.
Everything you need
is already inside you.

I felt my face flush.
I know lots of dazzling words,
but I've never written anything
big enough to hold
all the feelings in my heart.

≋

Soon as I walk through the door,
Ma asks me to trim the lantern wicks.
I won't get a chance to read—
or write—until after supper.

I don't tell Ma or Pa
what Miss Dowling asked
but I do mention the book of poems
by John Greenleaf Whittier.

Ma's eyes sparkle like lake stars,
but Pa just nods
and reminds me that it's fine
to read and copy words

so long as you understand
you can't pay bills
with pages from a book
and you can't weave a blanket
from pretty words.

I know Pa's right,
but books shelter me
in *downy* wings
and *whisk* me into
splendid worlds
where even the *indigent*
live as kings.

≋

After supper, Ma asks to see
the poetry book.
Before she opens it,
she studies the cover and smiles.

You'll have to take
good care of this, Willy.
A book is a treasure.
Miss Dowling is trusting you!

She slowly turns the pages.

I'm bursting to tell her
about the Decoration Day poem
Miss Dowling asked me to write.
But what if I can't do it?

Ma is always so proud of me.
I don't want to disappoint her.

Listen to this, Ma says.

"Slow fades the vision of the sky,
The golden water pales,
And over all the valley-land
A gray-winged vapor sails."

How beautiful is that?
No wonder you love words!

She reads me a few more lines
and finally gives the book back.

We'll have to work on your father.
Pretty words won't weave a blanket
but somehow they still keep us warm.

I've got to write something special.

For Miss Dowling.

For Ma.

But most of all, for Pa.
≈≈≈

MONICA FAGAN

Decoration Day is less
than a week away!
I asked Ma if I could
buy new ribbon
to brighten the trim
of my shabby summer shawl,
but I should have known—

The baby needs shoes, Ma says,
and Daniel's knee pants need patching.

She smiles at me.
Your shawl's in fine shape.
You take such good care
of all your belongings,
not like your brother.

What good is taking care
of things
if it means you never
get anything new?

Everyone in town
will be at the parade—
it would have been so nice

to have something
pretty to wear.

Now I'll look sorrier
than the saddest soldier.

≋

This morning at school
we practiced the poem
we'll recite at the cemetery.
Then Miss Dowling read us
another sad poem
about the rebellion.

Under the laurel, the Blue,
Under the willow, the Gray.

I'll be glad when
Decoration Day is over
and mornings start
with happy thoughts—
with sonnets by Shakespeare,
or stories about the past
and parts of the world
we've never seen.

Someday
I'm going to see the elephant—
everything—
I want to experience it all!

First I'll visit Ireland—
Ma says I've got cousins
I've never met—

then Italy—
Pisa,
where the leaning tower is—
and Rome,
to see the great sculptures
of Michelangelo
and the Colosseum,
where criminals
were thrown to the lions.

My brother Daniel's very lucky
he wasn't born in ancient times!
≋

GEORGE HOFFMAN

It's Saturday,
but Pa still leaves
early for work.
Ma's nursing Stella, so I get
Harry, Albert and Walter
washed and dressed
while Chrissie drowses
over jam and biscuits.

My friend Daniel says
taking care of babies
is women's work.
But my sisters
Lena and Lizzie
are already out of the house,
working as domestics.

Chrissie helps a lot
but she's only nine
and pretty scrawny.
Poor Ma looks ready to drop
even when the day's just starting.

If I could convince Pa
to let me quit school
and start working,
we'd have enough money
to hire our own help.

Then Chrissie
wouldn't have to act
like a grown-up
when she's barely
knee-high
to a bumblebee,
and Pa and Ma could
have a moment's rest.

≋

Tomorrow's Pa's only day off,
but after church,
he and a few other men
are taking a wagon
to that fancy club
on top of King's Mountain
to repair chipped bricks
and replace splintery boards.

When the season starts,
they'll remove horse slop
from the road leading to the lake.

It doesn't take a grown man
to remove horse slop.
It doesn't take an education either.

I need to work on Pa
so he'll let me get a job!

≈≈≈

JOE DIXON

Saturday wakes
to another grimy gray sky—
lucky for me,
news is more exciting
than weather.

I figure people will always
want to know
what's going on in the world,
and newspapers have it all,
not just business stuff
but odd and interesting facts—

the mother cat in Oregon
that adopted a squirrel,

the professor who fell from his horse
and forgot who he was,

the iron tower in Paris
that stretches higher
than five of the tallest trees—

Pa's got to understand
I didn't buy this newsstand

willy-nilly!
I have a plan!

Someday
I'll own a newsstand
in every train station
here and abroad!
≋

One of my customers said
most newsboys
never finished school
and can't even read!
Not me! I read
as many papers as I can—

The *Johnstown Tribune,*
the *Pittsburgh Dispatch,*
Harper's Weekly,
even the *Brooklyn Eagle.*

Already, I know
so much more
than I ever did,
so much more
than I'd learn
in the constant noise
and choking heat
of the foundry—

a loud, clanking place
that drowns out
noble thoughts
and burns away
bright dreams.

Maybe instead of selling papers,
you should write for them,

Maggie says.
You like to read.
You're good with words.
You care about people.
Everybody has a story.
Writing is a way
of honoring them.

Nah, I told her.
You'll see.
I'm going to be
a businessman,
like Andrew Carnegie.
≋

DANIEL FAGAN

I head to the bridge
to look for the bummer.
I want to give him
the lopsided star I whittled.

I am itching to hike the mountain,
but George has to help his ma,
and Willy has some secret
project he's working on

so my mountain exploring
has to wait.

Last year was our first
mountain adventure.

Large, leafy trees softened
the blazing heat of the sun
and blocked the factory soot
that trickled in the sky above us.

Was Willy who noticed
that the farther we climbed,
the cleaner the air
and bluer the sky
that peeked through the leaves.

Let's keep going, George said
when we reached the twin trees.

Lena and Lizzie are home
to help Ma with the kids.
I got a whole day
of peace and quiet.

We stopped to eat
the molasses cookies
Willy brought,
and take a swig from the
canteen slung over his shoulder.
Then we continued
into the unknown—

three bold explorers
venturing where nobody else
dared go.
≋

The bummer's not at the bridge,
so I skip rocks in the river
and I wish I were by the big,
beautiful lake
built into the side
of the mountain.

Last summer,
canoes and sailboats
drifted in water as blue
and sparkling
as the sky above it.
Spectacular, Willy said.
That water's shimmering
like a sea of stars!

Willy always talks like a book.
He wants to be a writer
when he grows up,
and Miss Dowling told him
it was never too early
to start collecting words.
George says if Miss Dowling
told Willy
to jump in the lake,
he'd do that too.

We watched boys
dive into the water
from a plank of wood,

laughing, splashing loudly,
calling out judgments
for each bounce and leap.

We should join them,
George said.

We can't! Willy argued,
pointing to a nearby
NO TRESPASSING sign.

There were signs everywhere:

SOUTH FORK FISHING & HUNTING CLUB,
MEMBERS ONLY.

LAKE CONEMAUGH, PRIVATE PROPERTY.

Willy looked to me for support,
but I was still deciphering what I saw.

Along the lake was a row
of houses with porches,
and boys and girls same age as us,
sitting in fancy Sunday clothes,
reading books
even though it was summer!

Some girls walked
the wood-planked paths,
carrying umbrellas—
parasols, Willy would say—
in the sunshine.
Other boys fished in the lake.

Somewhere the sounds
of a harmonica and banjo
floated above it all.

By the time I took it in,
George was sneaking
to the nearest porch
and crouching underneath.
≋

We watched quiet as spiders
till a pair of boots
blocked our view.

Get out now!
a raspy voice commanded.
We scrambled to our feet.

A man in work clothes and a vest
stood with arms akimbo,
his forehead wrinkled
and his bushy eyebrows sloping down.

I ever see the likes of you again,
I'll drag you to jail myself.
This here is private property.

Yes, sir, Willy squeaked.
We ran off and nobody
said anything
until we were halfway
down the mountain.

Willy found his voice first.
Did you see those boats gliding
around the lake
majestic as swans?
Spectacular! Sublime!

Even after we got caught,
me, Willy and George
climbed King's Mountain
all last summer.
We found a lookout
behind some bushes,
farther away but close enough
to hear the sound of laughter
and the clap of lazy oars
slapping the water.

My last rock skips five times
and I wonder why
some folks spend their summer
by a cool, crisp lake
while others stay home
scrubbing soot from their bones.
≋

WILLIAM JAMES

Finally, finally alone!
I pull out my notebook
and scan Whittier's poems
for words I might use
in a Decoration Day poem—

melancholy
somber
lonely
sober

I make a separate list
of words
I need to look up
in my Webster's dictionary—

vexed
vistas
furrow
persistence
guileless
blighted
forlorn
prodigal

The best way to learn
what words mean,
Miss Dowling says,
is to use them in a sentence.

With <u>persistence</u>,
Willy James will grow up
to be a famous writer.

I underline my new word
like I always do,

and hope what I wrote
comes true.

≋

Reading Whittier's poems
makes me think about Pa.

He never talks about the war
or what it was like to be a soldier,
but he walks with a limp,
and without his shirt on,
his misshaped arm is nicked
with holes and dents.

At least I survived,
he always says.
Most of my friends didn't.

Miss Dowling said that some
of the soldiers
were the same age as me
and my classmates
when they joined the army.

I try to imagine me, Daniel
and George
marching off to war together,
and Daniel and George—
or maybe none of us—
coming back.

Daniel and George are
like brothers to me.

We all live in narrow
wooden houses
on the same narrow street
just doors apart.

We walk to school together
every day.
Our three fathers work
long hours
at the Cambria Iron Mill
and come home every night
with the same hacking cough.

No wonder Pa never talks
about the war.

I can't imagine a world
without my friends.
≋

GEORGE HOFFMAN

Sunday's supposed to be
a day of rest,
but right after church,
Pa changes into his work clothes.

My sisters are home for the day.
Already, all the girls are sitting
in a circle sewing.
Already, Ma's reminding Lizzie
not to gossip,
and laughing at the stories
Lena tells.
Pa says Lena could tame
a grizzly with her funny tales.

Good to have you home, Pa says.
Lena, I'll miss your stories—
you'll have to retell them
at supper.
He looks at Ma. *I won't be late.*

It's now or never.
Pa, I want to get a job, I blurt out
right in front of everybody.
I can quit school—I already know
how to read and lots of men who
work at the mill never even—

50

G
E
O
R
G
E

H
O
F
F
M
A
N

Whoa! Whoa!
Slow down, son!
He looks at Ma
and they exchange
a glance
I can't decipher.

Then his large, strong hands
gently squeeze my shoulder.
We'll find some time to talk,
George, but for now
enjoy your sisters being home.

When he leaves,
Ma comes over
and kisses my head.

Why didn't I wait?
≋

Before Pa started
working at the club,
Sunday was my favorite day.
The whole family was together,
and after dinner,
Pa and I would walk
to our landlord's house.

Mr. Ryan's a widower
who never had children.
It was nice with everyone home,
but I still liked
walking alone with Pa
and visiting Mr. Ryan
in his calm, quiet house
without whining babies
or fighting brothers.

He must be lonesome, Pa said,
without the sound of children's voices.

Suddenly, Harry, Albert and Walter
tumble through the house
in a game of tag.

Think I'll check on Mr. Ryan,
I tell Ma. *See if he needs any help.*

Ma looks up from her mending
and smiles.
That's thoughtful of you, George.

*My little brother's turning into
a fine young man,* Lena says.
Pa's going to be proud of you!

Maybe this will show him
I'm ready to get a job.

≋

George! Come in!
Was just moving some furniture.
With the springtime rains,
rivers'll be overflowing soon.

Mr. Ryan's a real talker—
loquacious, Willy would say.
I guess that's because he doesn't
have anyone else to talk to.

Would you like some help?

Sure could use it.

We carry a table to the attic
and move a heavy,
cushioned couch
to where the table used to be.

It's not the seasonal floods
that worry me,
he continues.
It's that dam.
That dam's weak.
One of these days
it's going to burst.
James Quinn—
you know Quinn,
he owns the dry goods store

on Clinton—
Well, Quinn says
that dam bursts,
won't matter
where we move
this couch.
Ever see that big,
beautiful lake
in the mountain?

No, sir, I lie.

Any idea how much water's
in that lake?

No, sir.

Tons. Millions of tons.
Ever see the South Fork Dam?

I shake my head.

Know how old it is?

No, sir.

Old. From before the war.
No way to remove
surplus water either—

sluice pipes were sold
years ago.
Know what the breaches
are stuffed with?

No, sir, I don't.

Hemlock and hay.
Stumps and straw.
Mud and manure.

Mr. Ryan wipes his forehead
with the back of his hand.

That dam's one sagging slop.
It ever gives way,
Johnstown'll be wiped off the map.

Yes, sir.

Mr. Ryan nods for me to sit
while he carries a rocking chair
to a far corner of the room.
He's still talking.

They've been warned—
Carnegie and his cohorts
Frick, Mellon, Elder,
all those fancy members

of the South Fork
Fishing and Hunting Club—
they've been warned for years.
They just don't care.
Mark my words—
their self-serving folly
will destroy Johnstown!

He shakes his head.
Installing wire mesh
for their highfalutin fish!
Widening the walkway
to make room for their carriages—

My pa worked on that walkway.

A grand restoration it was—
ambitious,
swift—
and sorely incomplete!

He lowers his voice.
Long as the summer people
can swim and fish
and sail in the sunshine,
it won't matter.
They don't care a whit
about the likes of us.
That's the truth.

Yes, sir.

He nods me up and I help him
roll the rug beneath my feet
and drag it upstairs.
Thanks for your help, son,
he finally says.

Every spring, old-timers
worry about the dam
and every spring the dam holds.

Still, I take a deep breath
and shake off the swarm
of mayflies flittering in my gut.

What if this spring is different?
≋

GERTRUDE QUINN

After church,
Papa and Vincent
visit Grandfather
as they do most Sundays.
Grandfather has retired
but still likes to hear
all about the store.
Helen and Rosemary
sit on the porch, talking
and sewing *x*'s
into wooden hoops,
so I go upstairs
to play in my playroom.

Papa brought home
a pretend stove
that looks just like Mama's
and I have a table, chairs
and real porcelain dishes
that I keep in a cupboard
big enough to sit in.

*There's no need to be
cooped up inside,*
Aunt Abbie calls.
Go outside until supper.

Before she left,
Mama made me promise
to be extra good
and listen to Aunt Abbie.

She isn't used to spirited girls
like you, Mama said.
Please don't cause her
any trouble.
Be patient, kind and helpful.
LISTEN.

Remembering what Mama said,
I go outside without fussing
and hop to the hammock
on one foot.
Vincent's ducks honk hello
and I honk back.
Aunt Abbie's right.
No need to be cooped up!
≈≈≈

I jump off the hammock
and hop to the hutch
but it won't open.
Even standing on tippy toes,
I can't unlock the latch.

Helen and Rosemary
are so busy talking
they don't notice me
sneak back into the house.
Quietly, I grab the footstool
by the buffet
and spy the silver bell
Mama keeps on top.

A great idea
pops into my head!

In the bottom drawer
are strands
of leftover
ribbon and string.
I find a band
of black velvet,
unroll it
and carefully knot one end
around the bell.
Stool under one arm,
bell in the other,

I go outside again.

Where are you going, Gertie?
Helen asks without looking up.

Just nowhere, I say.

Stay out of trouble,
Rosemary says,
squinting at her needle.

I am staying out of trouble!
I plop the stool by the coop
and step on.
The latch is bent,
so I carefully untwist it,
open the door,
ring the bell
and toss it on the ground.

Wiggling the ribbon,
I march around the garden
with Vincent's ducks
waddling behind me
in a grand
springtime parade!

≋

Gertrude! Aunt Abbie calls.
Come inside this minute!
That bell you're dragging
around is an heirloom!
Your mother would not be pleased!

My mama wouldn't care.
She isn't sour and worried
all the time like Aunt Abbie.
Mama says people
are more important than things.

My fault, Vincent explains at supper.
I'm the one who told her
ducks like to follow shiny objects.

He and Papa look at each other.
Papa shakes his head and laughs.
I guess your fancy bent-latch design
doesn't deter intruders.

I told you nothing's beyond her reach.
Vincent laughs.
Leave it to our clever Gertie
to unloose a barred door.

With my mouth full of mashed potatoes,
I look at Aunt Abbie and smile.

≋

MONICA FAGAN

How's your new dress coming?
I ask Maggie on Monday
as we walk home from school.
Daniel's friends zip by,
and behind me
I hear Daniel's evil giggle.
He brushes my shoulder
and almost knocks me down.
'Scuse me. He laughs.

Spinning and walking backward,
he sticks out his arms and snaps
his scrunched fingers—
Chirp, chirp, chirp,
chirp, chirp, chirp!
Then he turns around
and sprints away.

You are so lucky
you don't have a brother,
I say, but soon as I do,
I'm sorry.
Maggie's father died
when she was little
and she's always wanted
a big family.
Tell me about the dress,
I say quickly.

I don't think I can finish it in time,
but anyway, it won't matter.
It's silly to wear something new
if there's mud puddles everywhere.

I look up.
Above us, dark clouds
hang in a gritty pitch.
Every spring, heavy rain
mixes with mountain runoff,
and swollen rivers
flood our street.
You're probably right.
Better get the buckets ready!

It isn't just the rain,
Maggie says.
Ma's worried about the dam.
Folks she works for say
every year it's worse
and dangerously closer
to washing away.
That lake
your brother loves to visit
won't be here forever.

Wait till I tell Daniel!
≋

Daniel isn't there
when I get home.
Probably looking
for that bummer.

Tell Daniel *not* to do something,
and he wants to do it more!

One of these days,
he's going to get himself
in real trouble
and it will serve him right.

Why should I
be the only one
who has to hurry
home from school
to help Ma?

Why do boys
own the world?
≋

Both babies are napping.

Ma sits by the window sewing
but looks up and smiles.

When summer comes, she says,
I'll teach you how to make lace
the way the nuns in Ireland
taught my mother.
Then someday
you can teach your daughter.

Ma is so old-fashioned—
no one wears
homemade lace anymore.
She should see
the beautiful fabric
and fancy trims
at Quinn's store uptown.
But she won't—
all she does is clean,
cook and sew—
why bother saying anything?

It's good to have traditions,
she says.
Besides, store ribbon
costs too much.

All you need for fancy
is a needle and thread.

She hands me
my summer shawl,
its ragged edges
hidden in threads
of dainty loops and swirls.

I'm glad I held my tongue.
≋

Maggie comes over after
I finish my chores
so we can practice
our lessons together.

I'm good at parsing sentences
and Maggie's good at ciphering,
so we make the perfect pair.

Since Ma doesn't need my help
with Clara or the baby,
Maggie and I
walk to the train station.
Joe Dixon, one of the boys
who's already graduated,
just set up a newsstand.

There's a line of customers
wanting Joe's attention,
so Maggie and I read
the headlines—

a rush for land in Oklahoma,
a new bridge in Pittsburgh.

Finally the last customer
tips his hat and leaves.

Maggie! Joe says. *Monica!*
So good to see you!

I laugh. The twinkle
in Joe's eyes
is for Maggie, not me.

Hi, Joe, I say,
and go on reading
about rich men
buying fields
of coal and iron
for poor men
to turn into steel.

≋

I scan the papers
for any news
of Ireland
to share with Ma,
but none of it is good.
Oppression.
Starvation.
Eviction.
Nothing about Ma's Ireland.

According to Ma,
Ireland's the most
beautiful place on earth—
everywhere the sweet scent
of heather and hay,
and lush fields
of green
sparkling brighter
than the sun.

Pa says Ma forgot
about the fields
of rotted potatoes
and the stench
of death and decay
that forced families
onto stinking ships
to find their way here.

No need to remind her,
he says.
Some memories are better
when they're dressed
in dreams.

It will take a lot of dreams
to dress up Johnstown!

JOE DIXON

One hundred fifty dollars?
How can a boy of fifteen
save one hundred fifty dollars?

I thought I found
the perfect moment
Tuesday after dinner
while Jacob and John
played marbles.
But Pa's steaming.

Have you any idea
what I would have done
with that much money?

Pa, I'm my own boss—
it's the cost of the newsstand
AND all the inventory.

What's wrong with
working at the mill?

I don't want to work
at the mill, Pa.
I don't want black breath
and aching bones.
I want to be my own man.

A man doesn't go chasing dreams,
thinking only of himself.
A man takes care of his family!

Pa grimaces and walks away.

Everything I want to say
catches in my throat
and I turn around quick
so Ma won't see me cry.

I squeeze the promise ring
still in my pocket.

Why can't Pa be proud of me?
≋

Even when I was little,
before Jacob and John
were born,
I knew I didn't want
to work at the mill.

For fifteen years,
Ma's spent her days
soaking,
soaping,
boiling,
wringing,
hanging endless laundry
on the line,
and Pa comes home,
shoulders hunched,
lunch pail empty,
his clean white shirt
foul-smelling
and blackened with soot.

But in books the teacher read
when I was younger,
there was another land

where the sky was always blue
and boats floated
in silver streams,
where homes echoed

happy singing,
playful voices
and laughter ringing.

Ever since I was little,
Pa's been coming home
too tired to laugh
and even in church
I've never heard him sing.

Ma says to give it time.
He'll come around.

I hope she's right.
I hope someday
he understands—

I just want to find
that place
of silver streams
and golden dreams.

≈≈

When I first started
sweeping floors
and stacking shelves
at the company store,
Pa was so pleased and proud.

Make sure you read
the framed words
posted in the back room, he said.
Mr. Morrell made that speech
when he was a congressman,
and he lived those words every day.
You'll never meet a finer man.

Mr. Morrell had already died
when I started working,
but his spirit lingered everywhere.
In his honor, we were encouraged
to respect each other
and take pride in our work.

The American workingman,
he believed,
must live in a house . . .
must wear decent clothes . . .
must eat nourishing food . . .
Industries operated
by American citizens
must be freed

from foreign interference . . .
and bind together
the whole people . . .

Whether we organized tools,
folded bolts of fabric,
counted change
or cleaned counters,
we did it Mr. Morrell's way—
neatly, cheerfully,
with a sense of humble purpose—

all important lessons
I plan to instill
in my own workers
when I have a business
of my own.

≋

DANIEL FAGAN

Wednesday afternoon,
Monica's chirping with Maggie,
and Ma makes me sort
her bottomless bucket of rags
before I can meet George.

Three piles, she says.
*For patching, for cleaning,
for tossing.*

If it were me,
I'd toss the whole bucket.
She should see the fancy cloths
girls at the club
use to polish silver.

Me, George and Willy
saw them last summer.
It was a hot day, but the club
was unusually quiet.
Only a few stragglers walked
along the water's edge
and no one
was swimming or sailing.

Must be the midday siesta,
Willy said.
That's nap time, he added,
looking at me.

Grown-ups take naps?

When they're hot, stuffed
and got other people
doing their dirty work, they do,
George said.
A wicked smile
crossed his face.
I dare you to look inside
the mansion.

I never say no to a dare.
Willy refused to come.

Maybe you'll see something
to write about, George said,
and dragged him
with us anyway.
≋

Quiet as Union soldiers,
we sneaked to the side
of the porch mansion.
The windows were just above
our sight, so we took turns
lacing our fingers together
to make a set
of tottery stairs to stand on.

Willie's the lightest,
so he went first.
Man alive! he said.
This place is magnificent!

Hurry up!
We don't have all day!

Willy jumped down
and shook his head.
Man alive, stu-pen-dous!

I stepped into his bony fingers
and steadied myself
by bending my knees
and clutching George's shoulder.

Legs balanced and braced,
I peered into a large room

with lots of tables covered in cloth,
and a brick fireplace
wider than my whole house.

Girls in white caps
and long white aprons—
Annie Butler and her sister,
Katie Downs, Rose Murphy
and two girls whose faces
I recognize from church—
skittered back and forth
carrying dishes,
folding cloths,
polishing silver with rags
cleaner than any in Ma's bucket.
≈≈

Willy's arm started quivering
and I jumped into the dirt.
My whole house could fit
in that fireplace! I said,
brushing my pants.
And all that silver—

Willy whipped a scrap of paper
and small pencil
from inside his cap.
—twinkling brighter
than sun on snow, he said,
scribbling madly.

And all those girls—

flittering like white moths.

Willy stuck his scribbles
back in his hat,
and we both wiped
our sweaty palms.

Your turn, I told George.

George shook his head.
Who needs to see a bunch
of two-legged moths
flittering around a fireplace
bigger than a house?

It's never worth arguing
with George
when he's in a sour mood.
But I understood how he felt,
and wondered why rich people
can't do anything for themselves.

In our house,
only babies take naps!
≈≈

GEORGE HOFFMAN

The bummer's not by the bridge.
So I convince Daniel
to hike the mountain.
I really need a breath of fresh air.

Daniel never says no to a hike.

We haven't even reached the first
PRIVATE PROPERTY sign
when we stop to rest
on a fallen tree,
its trunk so wide
we sit crossed-legged.

A big black ant crawls
along the bark
and I pick up a large leaf
to lift it and watch it
scrabble around.
Each time the ant
reaches the edge,
I turn the leaf over.

Do you know one of the big bugs
who comes here in the summer
paid more than ten thousand dollars
for a painting?

Daniel shakes his head.
A painting?

Yep. A painting
that just hangs on a wall.

The ant keeps reaching
the edge of the leaf
and starting over again.

We study him
without saying anything,
then Daniel uncrosses his legs
and stands up.
Come on, George, he says.
I can't watch that poor ant work so hard
and get nowhere.
Let's at least check the rock cave
before turning back.

I put the leaf and ant on the ground—
Good luck, little fella!
Go find yourself a crumb to eat!

A skinny tree blocks our path
and Daniel breaks off a branch
before jumping over it.
Perfect for whittling!

≋

The cave is really just
one big boulder
leaning on another,
but there's space underneath
wide enough to have a picnic.
Commodious, Willy said
first time we saw it.

When summer comes—
if I'm not working—
we're gonna camp here
and tell ghost stories.

Already, we stockpiled
three stumps for sitting
and an old, dented lantern
Ma said we could keep.
Now Willy can read the dictionary
before going to bed.
Daniel laughs.

Looks like someone's already living
in our commodious cave, I say.

Daniel uses his stick
to scratch the dirt
and a whole village
of small bugs
with shells on their backs
scuttles away.

I THOUGHT I TOLD YOU RUFFIANS
TO STAY AWAY!
THIS IS PRIVATE PROPERTY!

Daniel drops his stick
and we run—

Sign says Private Property—
Or can't you boys read?

It's the man with the raspy voice
and the bushy eyebrows.

I catch you here one more time,
I'll lock you up myself!
≈≈≈

When we're sure no footsteps
followed us,
we hold our chests,
breathe deep and sit down
on the fallen tree.

Daniel pounds the ground
with the heel of his shoe.
You can't own the woods!

He looked at us
like we were bedbugs.
What's a "roughen" anyway?

Daniel shrugs.
We'll have to ask Willy.

A spotted caterpillar slinks
across the rough bark.
Winged ants swarm
in a nearby stump.
An earthworm squiggles
through the dirt.

Let's get out of here,
I finally say.
Looks like rain.

By the time we reach Johnstown,
a few lazy drops are falling.

Where do you think
bugs go when it rains?
Daniel asks.
Do you think
they find
a place
to hide?

I don't know.
Maybe they
just drown.

≋

GERTRUDE QUINN

Finally! Tomorrow is Decoration Day!
Miss Wells reminded us to meet
at the cemetery after the parade.
Wear something red, white and blue
and remember,
tomorrow is a serious day.
No nonsense or rude behavior!

Last night at supper,
Vincent said the store's still busy.
We've less than a yard of bunting
and sold the last flag on a stick.
He winked at me.
Don't worry, I put one aside for you.

Hooray!!!
I love love love parades!

Streets crowded with watchers,
soldiers riding horses
or marching in a line,
wagons filled with flowers,
and best of all,
music that wakes up
all the happy feelings
I have inside me!

Finally, finally, finally!
Tomorrow is Decoration Day!
≋

In the afternoon,
Miss Wells's friend
Miss Diehl visits our classroom.
Miss Wells and Miss Diehl
were best friends at teacher school.

She's come to see the parade
and hear you sing tomorrow,
Miss Wells says.
And to make plans—
next month Miss Diehl
is getting married!
She looks at Miss Diehl
and smiles.
Even teachers
look forward to summer—
especially when there's
something to celebrate!

That gives me an idea!

Mama's birthday is in summer—
maybe we could have a party!

I love parties,
and Aunt Abbie will be so
impressed
by my thoughtfulness!

≈≈

After dinner,
I mention my big idea.

Can we have a party
for Mama's birthday?
We can have sugarcoated cookies
and ice cream and cake and candy
and string popcorn
like we do at Christmas
and hang sparkly ribbon—

Hmmm, Papa says,
Mama doesn't like
being the center of attention.

She'd tell us to save our pennies
for the poor,
Helen says,
and Aunt Abbie smiles.

And give the cookies to the hungry,
Rosemary adds.

I think it's a great idea, Gertie,
Vincent says.
We'll order the paper donkey game.
He tilts his head
and changes his voice.
For a jolly good time

and lots of fun,
the tailless donkey's
just the one!

We all laugh.

Please, Papa, I beg.
It will be so wonderful!

How can I say no
to the tailless donkey?
But not a word to Mama—
it needs to be a surprise.

I'm not very good
at keeping secrets,
but I promise
not to say a word.
This summer
will be the best one ever—
a grand party for Mama!

And Aunt Abbie
will finally see
how clever and thoughtful
I can be!

≋

WILLIAM JAMES

the river dark with <u>mortal</u> fear . . .
the hill range stood
<u>transfigured</u> in the silver flood . . .

My notebook is filling fast with
fancy words,
words I don't know,
and familiar, everyday words
strung together in new ways—

So many words and yet nothing
but scribbles and scratches
for Decoration Day.

If I don't finish my poem tonight,
I'll have nothing to read tomorrow.
I want to be a poet
like John Greenleaf Whittier.

I want to make people feel
the wet rain on my face
the cold snow in my hands
the lofty feelings in my heart!

But how?

≋

Brothers against brothers
beneath a leaden sky

~~*On bloody fields*~~
~~*under smoky skies*~~
~~*brothers*~~
somber
mournful
sorrowing
sad
mortal

I want to make Ma
and Miss Dowling proud—

I want to write
something
inspiring and meaningful,
something *meritorious*
enough to give Pa.

Pa was there. He knows,
he remembers.
I can only imagine.

I have only words,
and I can't find them.

Desperation creeps
between my bones.

≋

Who are you, fallen soldier?
I wonder.
I want to honor you,
but don't know how.

I turn to a clean sheet.
Who are you, fallen soldier?
I write.

I write.
I cross out.

I write.
I put back.

I write.
I cross out.

I cross out.
I put in.

I write.

Finally, I tear the cleanest sheet
from my book
and, in my neatest script,
copy the words
of my finished poem.

≋

JOE DIXON

At dinner, Jacob and John yap
about the parade tomorrow.
Pa tells them to settle down.
You best behave yourselves
at the cemetery, he says.
It's a solemn occasion.

Do you know who's speaking?
I ask,
but Pa goes on eating
like I'm not even there.

Ma shakes her head—
Let it go, her eyes beg.

Later that night she promises
Pa will be more responsive
when Decoration Day is over.
It's festive for the children,
she says,
but sometimes difficult
for the soldiers.
We honor them
by remembering
the very moments
they can't forget.

I'd waited
for the perfect
moment
to talk to Pa,
only it wasn't.
I hope I don't make
the same mistake
with Maggie.

But I can't wait
much longer.
Tomorrow
after the parade
and ceremony,
I'll take her aside,
slip the willow ring
on her finger
and ask her to be
my bride.

≋

DANIEL FAGAN

Where were you?
Monica asks
when I get home.
I hope you weren't snooping
around that club again.

I shrug my shoulders
and don't say anything,
but Meddling Monica
has a way of knowing stuff.

You did!
You did go to that club!
Wait until I tell Pa!

Tell me what?
Pa asks.

≋

ENOUGH!
NEVER EVER AGAIN!

Pa says if I know
what's good for me,
I won't go back.

Says if I get caught trespassing
ONE MORE TIME,
he'll let the owners
do with me
what they will.

Pa never yells.

My face burns,
my stomach drops.

If Monica wasn't such
a busybody,
Pa would never
have found out.

It's all Monica's fault!
≋

MONICA FAGAN

I don't know why Daniel
and his friends
sneak and snoop
where they don't belong.
It's not like I *wanted*
to get him yelled at.
Pa just walked in.

Still, it isn't fair—
Daniel disappears
for hours
while I'm stuck
at home
airing the bedding,
emptying the stove ash,
heating the sadiron,
folding the laundry,
sweeping the floors
and entertaining the babies!

I didn't want Daniel
to get in trouble,
but I'm not sorry that he is!
≋

That evening, Ma makes Daniel
do some of my chores
so Maggie and I
can practice our poem for tomorrow.

Can you keep a secret? Maggie asks.
She's sitting on the edge of my bed
while I brush and braid her hair.

You know *I can!*

Joe said Ed thinks you're pretty!

That's nice.

*Wouldn't it be wonderful
if I married Joe
and you married Ed?*

*Well, he'll be waiting
a long, long time.
I have too much
I want to do first!*

Maggie giggled.
*I know, I know,
but it's fun to think about,
isn't it?*

Thought you girls
were going to practice
your poem? Ma calls.

Maggie covers her mouth,
then in unison
we clear our throats,
straighten our backs
and enunciate each word
just like we practiced.

"The Vacant Chair,"
by Henry S. Washburn—
Maggie's so serious,
I start to laugh.

Again Ma's voice scolds—
Girls! More reverently!
This time,
I look straight ahead.

"We shall meet
but we shall miss him.
There will be
one vacant chair . . ."

≋

Maggie stays for dinner
and afterward I walk her home.
When I get back,
Ma's cleaning the kitchen,
Clara's rocking her rag doll
and Daniel is keeping
Tommy quiet—
by making a racket
with spoons and pots.

When he sees me,
Tommy waddles over
and grabs my leg.
Daniel squints
a savage glare.

I didn't tattle, Daniel.
Pa just walked in.

Daniel crosses his arms
and turns his back.

I sit beside him on the floor
and Tommy crawls into my lap.
Why do you and your friends
hike those woods anyway?

Because the sky
doesn't belong to them.

Who?

His arms still crossed,
Daniel turns toward me.
The summer people.
They think they're better than us.
They think they own everything—
the woods, the river, the sky.

Some people say the dam
that made that big lake
is old and ready to burst,
I tell him.
That private playground
won't last forever.
You're wasting your time
going there.

Daniel's scowl disappears
and his face pales.
If the dam breaks,
where will the water go?

Down the mountain, I guess.
More water for us to mop up.

That's a lot of water—

I don't know, Daniel.
It probably won't happen.

That dam's been here forever.
The point is, none
of those summer people
is more important
than you, or me, or any of us.
You're smart and funny
and someday you'll
have your own house
in the mountains.
Then you can put up
your own No Trespassing signs.

Never, Daniel says.
He uncrosses his arms.
Nobody can own a mountain.
His eyes flash like they do
when he's up to no good.
Well, maybe just one sign.

And what will that say?

Daniel's eyes twinkle.
MONICA, KEEP OUT!
≋

That night I tell Ma
that Maggie said
being with Joe
makes her feel giddy and happy—
like standing somewhere
high on a mountain,
close enough
to ride the clouds
and breathing only
clean blue air.
Do you feel that way
with Pa?

Ma laughs.
Maybe once,
but chores and children
pulled me back to earth
right quick.

I wonder how Ma would feel
if we had a house
in the mountains
instead of in this
soot-soaked valley.

≈≈≈

DANIEL FAGAN

At bedtime,
Pa's in the kitchen
hammering dents
out of Ma's tin pot.
Daniel! he calls.
Come here!

I get ready
for another blasting
about my trip
up the mountain,
but Pa gives me
a cleaning rag to hold.
His voice is soft
as a kitten's tail.
Look, he says,
the members of that club
are no better than you,
just like we're no better
than the vagrants
down on their luck.

My face burns,
remembering again
how I turned away
from the bummer.

But it makes no sense going
where you're not wanted—

they have enough signs
reminding you to stay away.

He takes the rag,
wipes down the pot,
then stops and
looks at me for a long time.
Your turn will come, Daniel,
he finally says.
Work hard.
Be patient.
Be kind.
Your turn will come.
In America,
you can be anything.

Well, when I grow up,
I say,
I'm going to be rich—
I don't know how,
but I'm going to be rich,
and when I am,
first thing I'll do
is take down
those No Trespassing signs.
The blue sky belongs to us all.

≈≈≈

MONICA FAGAN

I never thought I'd think this,
but Daniel's right.
People who have money,
who shop at fancy stores
and buy pretty things,
shouldn't think they're better
than folks who scrabble
and scrounge
and go to sleep tired
and hungry.

In this whole world,
there's nobody kinder
than my pa,
and nobody who works
harder than Ma.

Shouldn't that count
for something?
Shouldn't they have a chance
to rest?
To breathe fresh, clean air?
To travel around the world?
To laugh and dance
and have fun?

Shouldn't everybody
have that chance?

≋

I can't give Ma a cottage
in the mountains,
or the sweet smell
of heather and hay
and the lush green fields
she longs for—

but when Decoration Day
is over
and summer
finally starts,
I'll give her
the one and only
happiness
I can afford—

I'll let her teach me
how to make lace
the way the nuns
in Ireland
taught her mother.

And then someday,
when all my traveling
is done,
when I've visited
the green fields
of Ireland
and seen

the priceless treasures
of Italy,
I'll settle down,
get married
and teach my daughter
how to make lace
the way my mother
taught me.
≋

GERTRUDE QUINN

I lay in bed a long time
without sleeping
but finally tomorrow comes!

I jump up, mumble
my guardian angel prayer
like Mama says I should,

then get washed and dressed
for the parade.

Everyone is already awake
and downstairs.
Rain clouds darken the sky
and a misty rain falls.

Maybe heaven is crying
for all the soldiers lost
in the war,
Helen says at breakfast.

Aunt Abbie nods.
Perhaps so, Helen!
What a grown-up,
sensitive thing to say.

Helen is Aunt Abbie's favorite
because she never
causes any trouble.

I keep trying
to be like Helen,
but then
something
always happens
and I forget.

≋

Papa, Vincent, Helen and Rosemary
leave right after breakfast
but Papa tells me
to wait and go to the parade
with Aunt Abbie and Marie.

But, Papa, I protest.

Papa's forehead wrinkles.
Aunt Abbie needs you here.
He turns to Aunt Abbie.
*The parade passes right
by the store. We'll meet there.*

My eyes beg Vincent for help.

Don't worry, Gertie,
he says with a wink.
I'll hold on to your flag.

I take a deep breath
and follow
Aunt Abbie upstairs
to change Marie.
*How about this pretty dress
with red zigzags
across the bottom?* I ask,
pushing away my grumps
like I know Helen would.

Yes. And let's put blue ribbon
in her hair, Aunt Abbie says.

Marie fusses and cries.
Maybe she's crying
for all the soldiers
lost in the war, I say,
but Aunt Abbie ignores me.

How does Helen do it?
≈≈≈

I rummage
through all the ribbons
in the bottom drawer
of the buffet.

I can't find blue, I say
when Aunt Abbie
comes downstairs.

Aunt Abbie shakes her head sadly.
It doesn't matter, Gertie.
Your baby sister is sick.
Look at these watery eyes!
And her face—it's so flushed.
She sits on Papa's chair
and wipes Marie's nose.
There are tiny white spots
in her mouth too—
I think she has the measles!

Marie's face *is* red
and her eyes *are* watery,
but Aunt Abbie won't let me
get close enough
to see the spots in her mouth.

I'm afraid we won't be going
to the parade, she says.

Not going to the parade?
It's Decoration Day!
Nobody stays home
on Decoration Day!

≋

But I want to see Papa march!
I want to sing our song
and lay flowers
on the poor soldiers' graves!
I can walk to the store myself—
I know the way.

Gertie! I'm just as disappointed
to miss the parade—

But Papa will be looking for me—
Miss Wells is counting on me—

It's dark and rainy.
One sick child is enough.
Aunt Abbie's face is like a rock.
Before the day is over,
your papa, your sisters
and your dear brother Vincent
will be soaked and sorry!

But it's just MISTING!
I stamp my feet
like Mama says I mustn't do.

Gertrude! Aunt Abbie says.
I'm surprised at you!
Now be a good little girl
and fetch me
a clean blanket for Marie.

Holding back my tears,
I run for the blanket.

How does staying home
with a sick baby
honor dead soldiers?

Just wait till I tell Papa
Aunt Abbie wouldn't let me go.
She'll be the one who's sorry!

≈≈≈

DANIEL FAGAN

Ma's dressing Tommy,
and Monica's brushing
Clara's hair,
so I leave the house
to meet Willy
frog hunting
down by the bridge.

*Stay out of trouble
and be back before
the parade starts!*
Ma calls.

I will, I promise,
nodding solemnly
to Ma and Monica
but laughing to myself.

This is great
frog-hunting weather.

Tonight is going to be fun!
≋

WILLIAM JAMES

Pa leaves the table early
to get dressed in his uniform.
I'll see you at the parade,
he says, tapping my head.

Ma tells me I can meet Daniel
soon as I finish my chores,
and long as I meet her
at the firehouse
when the parade starts.
This is a solemn day, Willy.
Not a day for Daniel's silliness.
Make sure you stay neat.

My heart is thumping.
My stomach twitches and turns.

Are you feeling all right? Ma asks.
You haven't touched your corn bread.

Just excited.

Well, finish eating.
It's going to be a long day.
≈≈≈

I choke down the corn bread
and hurry to wipe the soot
from the windows
like I do every morning.

The poem I wrote
for the cemetery
is folded in my pocket,
but other words
turn in my head.

I want to scribble them
in my notebook
before I forget them.

Ma's right,
it's going to be a long day.

A long, soppy, wet day.

Mournful clouds hang real low,
I write,
and a somber gray veil
drapes the sky.

Even without trembling fife
and drums
calling us to remember,
I can easily imagine

the smoky fields
of Gettysburg,
the <u>billowing spumes</u>
of gunfire,
the great <u>multitude</u>
of bodies
<u>splayed</u> and scattered
like dry leaves.

It doesn't rhyme,
but maybe
it doesn't have to.
I can't wait
to come home
and polish it!

≈≈≈

GEORGE HOFFMAN

Wish I could go with Willy
to meet Daniel at the bridge,
but Ma asked me
to round up the little ones
and help get them ready.
There's so many of us,
we make our own parade!

*Maybe we should hire
some help*, I say.
Pa's been too busy
for our talk,
but I haven't given up,
and now I'm thinking
I should convince Ma first.

*George, we'd need a lot more
half eagles to hire help.*

*But we don't have to be rich,
just richer.
Lots of people hire a nanny
or someone like Lizzie
to dust and sweep.
If I quit school—*

Ma shakes her head.
Your father and I
want more for you
than a job at the mill.

Chrissie comes inside
with Albert screaming behind her.
Harry chased him into the mud.
I tried to stop them
but they didn't listen, and now
my favorite red-checked dress
is soiled.

Ma consoles Chrissie
while I take Albert
by his muddy hand
to clean him up.

Daniel's right.
Taking care of babies
is women's work.

I don't care what Ma says—
before today is over,
I'll talk to Pa
and insist I quit school
to get a man's job.

≋

JOE DIXON

Maggie and Monica decorated
my newsstand with bunting,
and people are still arriving
for the solemn holiday.

Papers say forty people injured
in a train wreck in Missouri.

Two horses killed by lightning
in Illinois.

There's riots in Oklahoma

and a smallpox epidemic
east of here in Nanticoke.

But rain or shine,
in every city across the land,
drums will beat
and soldiers march
in heartfelt remembrance.

*We should never forget
those who died*, Maggie said.
*Each of them had a story.
Each of them
is worth remembering.*

I touch the ring in my pocket,
and picture myself
walking with Maggie
to the Stone Bridge.

I'll get down on one knee,
slip the ring on her finger
and promise my undying love.

Purple clouds loom
in all directions.
Crowds of people
mill about.
But waiting
for the perfect moment
doesn't always work.
Today's the day.
I won't let
my perfect moment
be foiled.

≈≈≈

Soon as I hear the first drumbeat,
I close my newsstand
and walk to the cemetery.

Speeches are just beginning
when I arrive.

Pa's talking to a neighbor,
and Ma's standing
with Maggie's mother.

I spot Maggie huddled
with her class,
gesturing my brothers
to be still.
When she sees me,
she smiles.

Ed comes from behind
and jabs me in the arm—
You must be thinking about Maggie,
he whispers.
You're the only one here smiling.

I look around
at the somber townsfolk,

the weary men
in Union uniforms,

the sea
of flower-covered graves.

No matter how lucky I am,
I mustn't be oblivious
to the suffering around me.

Maggie taught me that.
That's why I love her.

≋

MONICA FAGAN

On the way to the cemetery,
Maggie and I stop to watch
a parade of soldiers
solemnly tromp
to the loud, lilting music.

A few men hobble out of beat,
their misshaped fingers
clutching ribboned walking sticks,
or pushing cane-back chairs
with large wooden wheels.

A gaunt soldier with crooked legs
nods to us as he limps by,
the arms of his Union uniform
dangling empty at his sides.

A wave of sadness
rolls over me.

I should have listened
more respectfully
to Miss Dowling's
morning poems
and vow
to be more solemn
when we recite
"The Vacant Chair."

≋

WILLIAM JAMES

A thin mist shrouds
the cemetery—

Miss Dowling nods
to me
and I step forward.

My heart thumps.
My hands shake.
My voice quivers.

I look at Ma
and then at Pa—

I pull my poem
from my pocket,
take a deep breath
and begin to read.

≈≈

Who are you, fallen soldier,
whose name I do not know?
Is your youthful dream of glory
buried 'neath a field of melted snow?

Do you hear our somber drumbeats?
Do you hear our sober song?
Do you feel our doleful heartache
that you are dead and gone?

We will not forget you, fallen comrade!
Though long years be washed away,
forever you are in our hearts
and forever there you'll stay!

I'm afraid to take my eyes
off my paper,
until in the solemn quiet

I hear
a weary
limping
shuffle
coming
closer.

When I look up,
Pa takes me
in his crooked arm
and cries.

≋

JOE DIXON

After the formal speeches,
Maggie's class recites a poem,
and William James reads
something he wrote himself.

His hands and voice tremble,
but if I wrote something
beautiful as that,
I'd shout it from the mountaintop.

Finally, the younger children sing,
and a solitary soldier
steps forward with his bugle.

He plays notes so slow and sad
even the sky starts crying.
≋

WILLIAM JAMES

Before we leave the cemetery,
Miss Dowling hugs me.
Willy, that was perfect,
so, so beautiful.
I knew you could do it!

Ma's beaming like the sun.

Even Daniel's impressed.
Man alive, Willy, that was good!
he says when I join him.
Like good enough to be in a book!

George agrees.
Willy, you're gonna be
a great writer
when you grow up!

All the way home I wonder
if this was how Whittier felt
first time he shared his words!

≋

MONICA FAGAN

Ugh! I should have known
the imp was up to something!

When it started to drizzle,
Ma said we best head home.
Daniel didn't fuss
and when we got here,
he cheerfully played
marbles with Clara.

After dinner
without anyone asking,
he happily amused Tommy
while Ma and I
cleared the plates.

He helped Pa move
the table and chairs
to put buckets
under the leaks,

and later that night,
after the steady rain
had lulled me to sleep,
he howled like a banshee
when his slimy pet frog
jumped across my face!

≋

GERTRUDE QUINN

Papa says Aunt Abbie was right
to keep me home,
so I am playing in my room
until I feel more *civilized*.

See, I promised you,
Vincent says,
coming upstairs
with a small cloth flag.

I don't want to see or talk
to anybody,
so he leaves the flag
on my dresser.

When I hear him
downstairs again,
I take the flag,
climb into bed
and am almost asleep
when Papa comes in
to say good night.
I love you,
my stubborn little angel,
he says,
kissing my forehead.

I love you too, Papa,
I whisper,
all my stubbornness
washed away
by sleepiness,
by Papa's
kind voice
and the comfy sound
of raindrops
dancing on the roof.

≋

*Often
in the spring,
mountain
tears
and drenching
rains
overflowed
my
tapered
banks.*

Though many
expressed
concern
for my
long-neglected
wounds,
in the mountains
the sun still shone,
and on the club's
private lake,
water
still glistened,
fish still jumped,
sailboats
still glided
graceful as gulls.

GEORGE HOFFMAN

It didn't rain too hard
during yesterday's parade
but I never got my moment
with Pa.

I was hoping
we'd have time today,
but night brought heavy
torrents—
and the streets are flooded.

Already, Pa's home
from work
but we're too busy
to talk—
moving stuff away
from windows
and doors
in case water leaks
through.

With everyone stuck
in the house,
inside wails are loud
as outside rain,

loud as Mr. Ryan's words
echoing in my brain—

That dam's one sagging slop.
It ever gives way,
Johnstown'll be wiped off the map.

That swarm of mayflies
flitter in my gut.

With the dark sky
hanging low,
and a dismal rain
falling fast,
it's harder
to shake them away.

What if?
≋

WILLIAM JAMES

Not much else to do today
but sit by the window
in the front room and write.

drenching
dreary
drowning
lashing
mighty
misty
pelting
scattered
swishing
surging
bleak
brooding
dense
dark
whirling
ominous
desolate
dusty
fearful
fretful
sad
mournful
sorrowing
rain.

≈≈

The Storm

Morning comes ~~in~~ wrapped
in a dark, ~~ominous~~ whirling mist.
Ominous clouds turn and twist.

O Johnstown sons
and Johnstown daughters!
May your fears disappear
in the ~~surging~~ brooding water.

Another poem!
Miss Dowling will be so proud.
≋

GERTRUDE QUINN

Already the streets are overflowing.

You need to apologize to Aunt Abbie,
Papa says at breakfast.
Dr. Lowman came last night
while you were sleeping—
Marie does have the measles.
There's no medicine for it,
but Aunt Abbie was right
to keep your sister
warm and rested.

I wasn't the one who was sick—
I could have walked
to the parade myself,
but I listen to Papa
and tell Aunt Abbie I'm sorry.

Papa heads to the store
to move boots and shoes,
feathered hats and fancy ribbon
to the top shelves.
Keep the children inside,
he tells Aunt Abbie.
If the water gets any higher,
I'll come back
and bring them to the hill.
That dam breaks,

not a brick
will be left standing.

Aunt Abbie looks at me,
shakes her head and laughs.
What a worrier your papa is.
No amount of water
could disturb this fine brick home!

Fear shivers down my spine.
I wish Mama were here!

≈≈

A rainy day is the perfect day
for a culinary masterpiece,
Aunt Abbie says,
reading Mama's cookery book
with Helen and Rosemary.
Would you like to join us, Gertie?

No, thank you, I say.
Cooking and baking do not
interest me at all.
I'd rather be outside
chasing ducks with Vincent.
The water in the street
is high as his knee!

Lovely idea, Helen,
I hear Aunt Abbie say,
and decide to do
what Aunt Abbie
would never let me do.

I unbutton my shoes,
take off my stockings
and slip outside.

Sitting at the edge of the porch,
I dangle my bare feet
in the cold water.

The stems on Mama's flowers
have disappeared
beneath the waves,
and the colorful petals
look like tiny lily pads.

The water's deep, Gertie,
Vincent calls to me.
Stay where you are!

I watch him follow his ducks
around the corner,
and wish I could go with him.
≋

MONICA FAGAN

Pa made Daniel
toss the frog outside
and said
he'd be finding him
a job at the mill
this summer.

Daniel looks
so contrite
that I almost
feel sorry for him.

Almost.

≋

DANIEL FAGAN

Even if it wasn't raining
cats and dogs,
I wouldn't be going outside—

Monica made such a fuss
about a silly frog
on her face
that I'll be lucky
if I ever
see my friends again.

≋

Following a day
of mournful marching
and rousing music,
I feel an uncomfortable
ache—

a heaviness,
a shift, a sway—
a subtle unloosening
of the mud and straw
patches
in the wall
that holds me—

GERTRUDE QUINN

GERTRUDE! GET INSIDE!
From nowhere, Papa appears,
grabs my arm and drags me inside.
This is not a game!
Go upstairs and get changed!

I have never heard
Papa so angry.
Quickly, I wriggle
into a dry dress
and stockings.
I'm buttoning my shoes
fast as I can
when Papa stomps
up the stairs.
Follow me straight to the hill,
he shouts.
He grabs Marie and
bounds back downstairs.
Don't turn around
or stop for anything!

With one shoe still unbuttoned,
I quickly follow him.

Rosemary and Helen take hold
of Papa's elbows
and step to the dirty water.

I'm right behind them
when Aunt Abbie
grasps my wrist
and yanks me
back inside.

Look at that filthy water!
she says.
*We'll wait in the nursery
safe and dry—*
*I don't know
what's gotten into your papa—
and poor baby Marie,
already so sick!*

I twist my arm
and jiggle
my shoulders,
but Aunt Abbie
holds on tight
and drags me
up the stairs.

Why am I always the one
stuck inside with Aunt Abbie?
≋

DANIEL FAGAN

It's raining hard.
Pa comes home
early from work

but there's not
enough buckets
to catch the leaks.

MONICA FAGAN

I grab Tommy
with one hand
and Clara
with the other,
trying in vain
to keep them away
from the plinking tins.

Pa and Daniel are moving
pots and pails—
while Ma scurries
after them
with commands
and complaints.

Even the rain in Ireland
is sweeter than the rain here.
≈≈

JOE DIXON

Maggie went home yesterday
before I could pull her aside.
The promise ring still burns
a hole in my pocket,
and my heart is like the sky,
a dark, twisting tunnel of longing.

Yesterday's harmless drizzle
has turned into a drenching.
All night the rain
bucketed down in torrents.

Still, I thought if just one
customer stopped by,
I'd be here with a smile
and a kind word.

I thought Pa would see
I've got what it takes
to be a successful businessman
and prove myself worthy
of his pride.

But the streets are flooded,
and a successful businessman
has more sense than to stand
in water and sell wet papers.

I open my trunk to stow
whatever's not yet soaked.

I'll head home and help Pa
move Ma's sewing table
before I check
on Maggie and her mother.

I could give her the ring
at her house today,
but the rain's so heavy
and loud,
all my loving words
would be washed away.

≋

WILLIAM JAMES

Pa asked me to help
roll some rags
and stuff them
under the front door
so the rising water
doesn't seep inside,
but now I'm back
at the window.

Best get your writing
done now,
Pa said.
By the time
this rain stops,
we'll have a
slopping mess
to clean up.

The way the sky is *bawling*,
I'll have a whole book of poems
by nightfall.
≋

GEORGE HOFFMAN

Pa left to check on Mr. Ryan
and I wish he'd get back.
Water's rising in the street—
if he doesn't come home soon,
the water will be too high
to slog through.

Stay away from the window,
Ma says,
and you won't worry so much.

It isn't just the rain, Ma.
Mr. Ryan says—

I know what Mr. Ryan says,
Ma scolds.

Ma doesn't scold.

I sit beside her on the couch
and her voice softens.
She puts her arm around
my shoulder.
Let's not frighten the children, George.
They need our courage.

She tries to sound brave
but I can tell
Ma's just as scared as me.
≋

crushing
rain
continues
throughout the day,
roiling the roots
of my feeder rivers,
overflowing
weary banks,
weighing
heavily
on the decaying walls
that restrain me

by late afternoon
I feel a drop—
a shove—
and finally,
a desperate lunge
into chaos.

PART

T W O

WILLIAM JAMES

~~Frightful~~ thunder
sounds
in the distance.
Mournful ~~water~~ tears
~~weeps falls~~ fall
from the sky.

Somewhere the sun
is shining.
Somewhere the streets
are dry.

But here in this lonesome valley,
here in this ~~sorrowful~~ <u>forlorn</u> vale,
~~Sadness clings~~
the sky drips a mortal sadness
and trembles in the gale.

≋

GERTRUDE QUINN

From the third-floor window
I see a rush of people
running through the street.
I hear their terrified screams,
and the loud crackle
of falling timber—

Church bells chime.
The mill whistle shrieks.
Aunt Abbie screams.
My heart bounces
and my stomach spins!

A mountain of darkness
rushes and rolls
on the scramble below
like the sky itself
is chasing them,
like the sky itself
is coming down,
dragging with it trees
and houses.

Aunt Abbie looks at me
with wide,
frightened eyes
and kneels to pray.
The house rocks—
the ceiling falls—

In a thunderous
crash and crack
walls collapse
floorboards burst—
water gushes up
and pours in
from every side.

It's the end of the world!
Aunt Abbie cries.

≈≈≈

My mouth fills
with water
and wood.
Papa! Papa!
I scream

choking,
spitting—

Why did you stop me,
Aunt Abbie?
Why didn't you let me
follow Papa?

Cold water
swirls around me.

Papa! Papa!
I call—

all the while knowing
he cannot hear me.

≋

GEORGE HOFFMAN

The water bursts
through the front door
and quickly rises
to the top
of the dining table.
I wrap Walter
around my neck
like a scarf,
and lift Stella
into my arms.

With Harry, Albert
and Chrissie
clutching her skirt
like a frightened
litter,
Ma hastens us
first to the attic,
then to the roof.

Stella cries,
but Walter buries
his face in my shoulder
and holds on tight.

His skinny fingers
feel like a family
of cold, wet worms
crawling on my neck.

≋

Trees, wooden planks
and a whole barn
float on the water below.
People hang off boards—
some kneel,
some pray,
others clutch animals
and call out for help.

Ma takes Stella into her arms
and she stops crying.

Walter digs his fingers
deeper into my neck.

That's Mr. Musante!
Harry says. *The fruit man!*

Chrissie turns
her head to peek
at the mustached man
skittering by
on a narrow door,
fearfully clutching
his family and
an opened trunk.

Where are you, Pa?
Lena? Lizzie?
Where are you?

≋

WILLIAM JAMES

roaring
raucous
rushing
rousing
rumb
≈≈

MONICA FAGAN

The streets are flooded
and water's leaking
through the walls.
Ma grumbles about living
in a soggy tinderbox
but Pa begs her to stay calm.
The rivers have flooded
the streets before, he says.
We'll get through this.
Things'll get better.

When, Matty, when?
Ma argues.

Before Pa can answer,
a terrifying roar—
a crashing
thrashing
rolling rumble
silences Ma
and frightens all of us.

We huddle together—
Ma holding Tommy
and Pa holding Clara.

Hail Mary, Ma prays—

Full of grace,
we mumble.

Pa bows his head,
Daniel and I
look at each other
and grasp hands—

now and at the hour—
≋

DANIEL FAGAN

Raging water
and tangled wire
whisk away
our roof and walls.

Jagged wooden claws
force apart my family.

I grab a mangle
of tree and twisted metal
and quickly lose sight
of Ma, Pa and the babies.

Nearby, Monica rides
the dark,
cluttered wave
on a narrow,
sludgy floorboard.
I call to her,
but my voice
is lost in a chorus
of shrill screams.

Something catches the wire
of my ragtag raft,
and when I look up,
Monica is gone.

≋

JOE DIXON

I heard it before I saw it—

a monstrous bellow
threatening
angry
shattering—

and then,
floating toward me,

a violent wave
of fallen trees
and flattened
houses—

a swelling,
cannon-like roar—

a furious surge
of rubble-filled water

that topples
my newsstand

and pulls me
under its angry swirl.

Driftwood and wire
tangle around me
and a ferocious fear
fills my lungs.

I'm pushed into the air—
dragged back beneath the filth—

a breath—
a plunge—
a breath—
a plunge—

all around me
nothing
but wood,
wet,
slime
and darkness.

≋

GERTRUDE QUINN

The nursery's filled
with water,
darkness
and loud ghostly gurgles.

Aunt Abbie's sobs
and prayers have stopped
and there's no answer
when I call her name.

A coldness,
like the coldness
of the water,
blankets my heart.

I am here all alone.
≋

MONICA FAGAN

Clutching a broken
floorboard,
I ride the massive
wall of rubble.

Around me,
houses
and buildings
crumple
like paper bags.
I bump
against wagons
and train cars,
doors, rooftops
and other floating trees.

The water's swollen wrath
threatens to pull me under,
but I hold on tight,
frantically searching
the twisted wreckage—

desperate to find
Ma, Pa and the babies,

desperate to find
my brother Daniel.

≈≈≈

JOE DIXON

Unable to struggle
any longer,
I close my eyes
and let my arms
hang loosely
at my side—

suddenly, a hand
reaches down
and pulls my face
out of the water.
I cough and kick my feet—
Edward!

My friend slips his arms
under my shoulders,
drags me through
the watery wreckage
and drapes my body
across a toppled tree
stretched
between two houses.

*I wasn't so sure
you'd make it,*
he says.

I'm not so sure I have.
≋

GERTRUDE QUINN

The water gurgles and swirls
but doesn't swallow me.
A drop of light
flickers somewhere above.

Holding my breath
and stretching
my head back
to stay above water,
I grope and thrash
my way toward
the shimmering speck.

Something solid scrapes
my legs—
I shinny up a soggy piece
of wood
and squeeze through
a narrow opening
that leads outside.

Around me, angry water
ripples and roars.
Below me, Mama's quilted
mattress bobs in the waves
like a magic carpet.

I call out to her and jump.
≋

Mama's mattress totters
and tilts,
and I teeter-totter
from side to side,
to keep
from going under.

Broken beams
and wagon wheels
fallen trees
animals and people
tangled in wire
swirl around me.

Help! Help!
Somebody please help,
I call.
But nobody answers.

My body shivers
in the growing
dark and cold.

Ever this day, be at my side,
I pray, over and over
repeating the same line
from the guardian angel prayer
I say every morning,

not remembering
any other words.

Ever this day, be at my side.
Ever this day—
≋

A small house floats by
with an old man
clinging to its chimney.

Please help me, I beg,
but the man stares ahead
like a statue.

Then another man,
a younger man,
jumps into the water.

His head bobs
up and down,
so one moment
I see him
and the next
I do not.

Ever this day be at my side,
I pray, hoping to see
the man's face
bob again
above the water.

≋

MONICA FAGAN

Snagged by the ruins
of the Stone Bridge,
I hear my name called.

Ma! Pa!

Nearby, still holding
the babies but caught
in the wicked embrace
of two crossed beams,

Ma and Pa huddle
together,
more anguished
and sorrowful
than a statue
by Michelangelo.
≋

DANIEL FAGAN

Houses, trees and train cars
swirl around me!
My raft twists and twirls
in the muddy current
and swallows my cries
for help.

The restless water
pushes me
toward the bridge
where I found my frog,
and for a moment
I wonder about the bummer
who taught me to whittle.

What has become of him?

What has become of Ma,
Pa,
Clara,
Tommy,
Monica?

What will become
of me?

≋

The rushing current
deposits me
in a great
tangle
of people and debris
piled at the bridge.

I adjust my eyes
to the wet murk
and search
for the faces
of my family.

Moments later
the bridge is in flames.
≋

GERTRUDE QUINN

The bobbing man
makes his way
to my quilted raft.
I've got you now, little one,
he says,
lifting me into his arms.

Together,
we bump and bounce
in the cold water
until we reach
the bottom of the hill.

Two men stand
in the upper window
of a little white house,
holding out a long pole.

People close enough
and strong enough
to grab the pole
are pulled to safety.

I stretch out my arms
but am too far away.

Throw that child over,
the men at the window shout,

and I feel myself
tossed into the wet air.

Be safe, the bobbing man
calls after me. *Be safe.*

Wrapped in wet,
tattered
darkness,
I wonder
what that means.

≋

Landing in the arms
of another stranger,
I'm wrapped in a blanket
and carried up a hill.

Voices call out—
the stranger
stops moving
and draws
the blanket
from my face.

A crowd of people
peer at me
like I've been dropped
from a cloud.

Who is she?
Don't recognize her—
So young!
Poor thing!

Someone pulls the blanket
back over my face
and the stranger
who carries me
starts walking again.

Maybe I *was* dropped
from a cloud—
there is no one here
who knows me.

I do not know myself.

≈≈≈

The walking stranger
stops again and places me
in someone else's arms.

Poor thing, a woman says.
She carries me inside a house
with lots of children
and gently unwraps me.

Go to the attic for the flannels,
she tells one child.
*Fill some mason jars
with hot water,* she tells another.
This poor little girl is freezing!

The woman dresses me
in itchy red flannels
and looks at me with
kind mother-eyes.
What's your name?
she asks softly.

Words bounce off me
like I'm made of stone,
and I think of the old man
who floated like a statue.

Finally, one of the children
leads me upstairs.

Mama will take good care of you,
she says.

Mama. A fading word
from far away.

Where are you, Mama?
Where are you, Papa?

Where am I?
≋

My body aches to sleep
but I'm too scared
to close my eyes.

I'm afraid to see
animals and people
tangled in wire.

I'm afraid to hear
loud crackles
and shrill screams.

I lay still a long time,
then kneel on the bed
and look outside.

Across the water,
fires blaze
like lost ships
flickering
in a lonely sea.

I keep my eyes open
and watch them burn.

≋

DANIEL FAGAN

All through the night
the flames grow closer.

I feel the heat,
taste the kerosene
and join my voice
to the maddening
shrieks
that surround me

until

one by one,

the heat

the smell

the shrieks

all stop.

≋

PART

THREE

Lake emptied,
rain dwindling,
ravished rivers
retreat
to torn
and muddy banks,
the violent,
rushing
torrent
leaving in its stead

an eerie,
silent
wasteland,
a desolate wilderness
littered
with
uprooted trees
and twisted tracks,
crushed train cars,
toppled buildings
and
lost,
lifeless
bodies.

JOE DIXON

Morning arrives shimmering
with shock and sorrow,
her face still wet with tears.

The soot-filled town
I longed to escape
is battered now,
mangled and mute—
the clanking
of the mill,
the train whistles
and church bells,
the clopping of workhorses
on cobblestone streets
all shattered now—
silent.

At the Stone Bridge,
a smothering fire burns
and the air reeks
with the smell
of smoke and rot.

Slowly, we who survived
stagger to our senses.

Draggled and weary,
we scour the wasteland,

searching for those we love.

≋

A desolate, damp haze
settles in the valley.

The few buildings
left standing
look like toothless,
gaping giants
towering
in a lost
kingdom
of water,
mud
and rubble.

The ring I made
from willow twigs
is gone, but
the promise remains

and somewhere
in this wasteland,
people I love wait
for me to find them.

≋

GERTRUDE QUINN

Wet darkness drips
into gray dawn.

I sit on a porch.
Other people also sit.

Their faces are scratched.
Their hair is wild.
Their clothes are ill-fitting,
too large or too small.

Someone asks,
Aren't you little Gertrude Quinn
whose father owns Quinn's store?

My heart skitters but my voice
stays trapped inside me.

The stranger-voices
whisper and buzz.

What do you think?
It looks like her—
maybe not—

If we removed the sticks
and mud from her hair—

and combed it—

Isn't that her aunt
making her way over here?
≋

GERTRUDE

QUINN

Aunt Barbara climbs
the porch steps
and someone calls her
to my side.
I feel her touch my face.
I feel her stroke
my knotted hair.

Yes, yes! It's Gertrude!
I hear her say.
Gertie, it is me—
Aunt Barbara!
What happened, Gertie?
I thought I saw you
follow your father
out of the house.

I feel her arms around me.
I feel her kisses
and her tears.
I hear her soft words.

But I am a block of wood,
a broken branch,
a floorboard tossed
and battered
in dark, cold water.

≋

JOE DIXON

Miraculously, I find
Ma, Jacob and John
huddled on a plank
wedged between
two sagging houses—

Ma cries when she sees me.
Jacob clutches my arm,
and John buries his head
in my shoulder.

He's gone, Joe, Ma whispers.
*We saw the water rise
and carry him away.
What will we do?
How will we manage?
I can't move my leg.*

A wet chill washes
over me—
my father gone?

I never had the chance
to prove myself,
to please him—

Again, I'm plunged
beneath cold water,
unable to breathe.
≋

Strangers help carry Ma
to a once-splendid home
battered but still standing
and hastily transformed
into a temporary hospital.

She'll walk with a limp
the rest of her days,
the doctor says,
but there are injuries far worse.

Through a watery fog
I hear Pa's voice
as firm and strong as if
he stood beside me.
A man doesn't go chasing dreams.
A man takes care of his family.

I gently squeeze
my mother's bruised hand.
I'll take care of you, Ma.
I promise. I'll take care of you.

I kiss my brothers'
bedraggled heads.
You need to stay here with Ma.
Look around you. Be helpful.
People are suffering.

Both boys are wide-eyed and silent.

I need you to be strong.
I'll be back before nightfall.
Maggie and her mother
might be trapped
in the rubble.
I've got to find them.

I don't for a moment
let myself consider
what I might find.

≋

GERTRUDE QUINN

In the still early
morning,
I see Papa run
toward the house,
his collar open,
soap lather stuck
in his whiskers.

I fly off the porch
and into his arms.

My little one, he cries,
my precious little one!

I whimper like a lost kitten,
but words
stay trapped inside me.

Papa buries his wet face
in my tangled hair.
Never, never again
will I lose you!

My wooden bones
begin to quiver.
Please, Papa, I whisper,
hold me!
Please don't let me go!

≈≈≈

B-84

I never let go.
Even when those skinny
wormlike fingers pulled
and pinched my neck,
I never let go.

Even when their shrill
screams pierced my ears
and the furious wave
washed over us,
I never let go.

I only wished
I hadn't strayed
so many times before.

Now cries are muffled
by lace-edged cotton,
the sound
so soft, so mute,
one barely remembers
the tumult—

the clutch of skinny fingers
loosened now
but still wrapped
around my heart,
invisible,
but strong as spider's silk.

≈≈

G-130

So engrossed in finding
the perfect word
for my poem,
I did not see or hear
the monstrous wave

until it burst
through window and wall

and smothered me
in its savage embrace.
≋

(-49

When the shrieking
stopped,
when the air opened
endless
and clear,
I floated above
the scorching fire
and surging flood.

I saw the brightest light

and followed it.

≋

CLARA BARTON

There are times
when words
are insufficient
and only action matters.

I tended the wounded
at Antietam, Bull Run
and Cedar Mountain.

In Andersonville,
I searched
for the missing
and tenderly
marked their graves.

Now I place
my beloved
Red Cross
above the weary
wreckage
of Johnstown,

determined
to plant hope
in this quagmire
of despair.

≋

C-47

Life was going to be so grand!
I had so many dreams—
the lush green fields
of Ireland,
the grand sculptures
of Michelangelo—
all the wonders of the world
that I longed to see
before settling down
and finding love.

On a night before the flood
I was rocking Tommy
in the dim light
of a flickering lantern.

He had fallen asleep in my arms
and tenderly, with rough,
onion-smelling hands,
Ma lifted my chin and smiled.

*You asked if being with Pa
makes me feel giddy and happy,*
she said.
*Love's a little like water.
It's got many moods
and takes many shapes.
But it's a beautiful gift*

that shouldn't be taken
for granted.
Just wanted you to know
I'd rather be rooted
in the soot of Johnstown
than standing
on a mountaintop
with anyone
other than your pa.

For now and for always,
love lies not in hope
but in memory.

≋

C-46

The great famine
chased my family
from Ireland
to America,
and a heaving sea
hastened my birth
on an overcrowded ship.

It is true what they say—
what I tried so hard
to teach my son—
work hard and
your turn will come.
America is the land
of opportunity.

If he ignores
the taunts,
and closes
his tired eyes
to the bigotry,
a child
born with nothing
and clothed in rags
can grow up
fearless and strong.

So I believed
before the waters
washed away our home
and the flames
devoured my family,

so I believed.

≋

C-48

Oh, Matty!
You tried so hard
to provide for us—
all your life
working against
the shame
of poverty
and the stigma
of torn roots.

In a country that favors
its native-born,
you believed hard work
would prove us worthy
to be here.

When I grumbled against injustice,
you promised me better days.

When I complained
of living in a tinderbox,
you wrapped me
in your muscled arms
and reminded me
our family was our shelter.

How fitting, my dear Matty,
that we should perish together!
I should have told you sooner
how very much I loved you.

≋

JOE DIXON

Day after day,
survivors
search
the ruins.

Hungry, cold,
dazed and tired,
I slosh
through mud

and scrabble
toppled buildings.

Using crude tools,
I scrape and dig,

I hope.
I pray.

No sign of Pa
or Maggie,
but there are
so many others.

≈≈≈

Without wagons or horses,
bodies are carried
through the mud and sludge
to shattered buildings
turned into makeshift morgues.

Doors, floorboards
or whatever planks
of wood can be found
are used for transport.

Pockets are emptied,
rings and brooches
removed,
each body cleansed
and tagged,
their names
or descriptions
recorded
on whatever scrap
of paper
can be found.

Without tears
or raging grief,
as if my heart
were cased in glass,

I find Pa in a field
near the railroad.

I find Maggie
at the schoolhouse
on Adams Street—

two beloved souls
among the hundreds
who wait to be identified.

≈≈≈

C-273

I was employed
by the Cambria Iron Company
and worked my way
from machinist to engineer.

Hoped the same for my boy, Joe,
but he had other ideas,
dreams of finding his own way,
being his own boss.

I didn't want to
discourage you, Joe,
but life is hard,
and I didn't think
you'd ever find
a more promising workplace.

Still, I wish I'd told you.
Wish I'd found the words to say
I love you.
I want you to succeed.

Even if your way
wasn't my way,
even if your dreams
weren't my dreams,
I was always proud of you, Joe.

≋

A-143

I know it was hard,
but I'm glad you found me
before Ma did.
She's suffered enough
taking care of Pa,
and when Pa died,
taking care of me,
cleaning other people's houses
and wishing life were different.

Even when I was little,
I told her
when you and me grew up,
we'd get married
and have lots of children.
You'll never be lonely again,
I promised.
Told her we'd build a house
in the mountains
with a room just for her
where she could rest
her sore back
and see puffy white clouds
instead of floating bursts
of soot and grime.

I know you're heartbroken, Joe,
know you got your own family,

your own burdens,
your own business to care for,
but I hope you'll remember my ma.
She'll be missing me
and our house in the mountains,

and all the children
you and me never had.

≋

A-135

What fun we had reminiscing
about our days
at the Normal School
preparing to be teachers.

What excitement, Jennie,
as we imagined the joy
of my upcoming wedding.

And my dearest, William,
how tenderly you wept,
when you claimed
my lifeless body—

how gently you placed
your gold ring
on my cold finger.

≋

A-146

In school,
we were the best of friends,
inseparable
as blue from a summer sky.

Just days ago, walking back
from the schoolhouse,
we linked arms
and played our favorite
end-of-the-day game.

Best moment? I asked.

Hearing the young ones
sing their hearts out.
Especially that girl
with the cropped hair—

That's Gertrude.
Lively little Gertrude.
She pours her heart
into everything.

Well, she certainly
has a vigorous voice.
If any of your students

leave a mark
in this world,
it'll be Gertrude.

I'm counting on you, Gertie.
I'm counting on you.

≈≈≈

GERTRUDE QUINN

A few days after the flood,
Rosemary, Helen and me
wait on line for petticoats,
stockings, smocks and shawls
donated by kind strangers.
All the fancy wraps
in Papa's washed-away store
could not warm me as much
as my new breakfast shawl.

Slowly, my wooden limbs
soften and unbend.

Vincent has not been found,
but Papa says
there may yet be survivors
trapped beneath the rubble.
Do not give up hope! he says.

I pray harder for Vincent
than I even prayed for myself.
≈≈≈

We move to a building
with other families,
and a white flag
with a big red cross
flying above the door.
Papa says the little woman
with the dark eyes
and muddy shoes
who welcomed us
is building Red Cross hotels
all over Johnstown.
Not real hotels,
not like the fancy new one
that washed away,
but quick-built places
where people would be safe and dry.

Things will get better,
Papa promises.
Uncle Edward is coming
to bring you to Scottdale,
and relief money will soon be
distributed according to need.

We're going to Scottdale?
I can't wait for Mama
to scoop me in her arms.
Soon, Vincent will be found—
and my whole family
will be together again!

≋

The very next day,
when Papa comes back
from his daily search,
we run to him as we always do.

Papa hugs all of us at once—
but then, instead of kissing
each of us on the forehead,
he draws us closer.

Your brother's been found,
he whispers.

Papa's shoulders tremble
and he bows his head.
When he raises it again,
red-rimmed eyes
tell us what his words do not.

Vincent, my brave big brother
who I loved so dearly,
who cheered away my tears
with smiles and small treasures,
who let me play with his ducks
and never teased or scolded me,
was caught
in the treacherous current
and lost forever.

I cling to Papa before I float away.
≋

A-195

I played with the ducks
and warned Gertie
not to follow me
into the deep water.
Dear rambunctious Gertie!
I loved your feisty spirit
and knew you'd follow
me anywhere!

The ducks flapped and flew
as if it were a game,
but I grew tired of chasing them
in the quickly rising water—

Suddenly, church bells
chimed wildly,
train whistles
shrieked madly.

With my mother away,
I worried about my sisters,
especially Gertie.
Had she gone inside?
Was she safe?

The water almost reached my neck
and was running swiftly—

On the corner
of Main and Bedford,
just a few doors
from home,
a great wall of water
pushed me,
and a strong crosscurrent
pulled me under.

I should have gone home sooner!
≈≈≈

JOE DIXON

Within days, help arrives
from all corners
of the country—

four hundred bushels of wheat
from Kansas,

twenty thousand hams
from Cincinnati,

tents for the homeless
and financial
benevolence
from Boston,
Brooklyn
and beyond the sea.

Boxes and boxes.
Bushels and bushels.

But none of them filled
with bandages
to swaddle broken hearts.

≋

Doctors and nurses also arrive.

A little lady
with pulled-back hair
and a plain black dress
sets up an office
in a broken-down rail car
and with a team of volunteers
takes charge of everything—

assessing the needs
of each survivor,
providing temporary housing,
distributing supplies,
offering medical care
and comfort.

Daily, her rickety buckboard
rattles through the streets,
an almost-forgotten relic
of normalcy and progress.

≋

CLARA BARTON

At first, I am misunderstood—
considered a poor,
helpless woman
in need
of man's assistance.

But when tents are assembled
and lumber arrives,
when food is distributed
and shelter constructed,
minds change,
and my mission becomes
unmistakably clear:

In times of crisis,
whether young or old,
woman or man,

we must heal the broken
and comfort
the heavy-hearted.
≋

JOE DIXON

Newspapermen come too—

reporters and artists
seeking to record the disaster
in words and sketches
that keep donations pouring in—

loaves of bread baked daily
by prisoners in Pittsburgh,

clothes, bedding and Bibles
in boxes marked
FOR THE JOHNSTOWN SUFFERERS,

and when rail service
is finally restored,
train cars
full of coffins
large and small.

≋

B-67

Some say
the flood
was punishment
for our
wickedness—
our laziness—
our greed.

I worked
at the mill
twelve hours
a day,
six days
a week.

I provided
for my growing
family
and checked in
on our widowed
landlord
whenever I could.

Where, I ask,
was my
wickedness—
my laziness—
my greed?

≋

A-17

What more could I have done?

For years Morrell begged them
to fix the dam properly—
even offered to help pay
the cost of repairs—
even became a club member
to keep an eye on things.
But rich and influential
as he was, Morrell's pockets
weren't deep enough.

What, then, could I have done,
my own pockets empty
as a soaker's cup, taking in boarders
to pay my mortgage?
That dam's one sagging slop,
I'd say to anyone who'd listen.
It ever gives way,
Johnstown'll be wiped off the map.

Sorrow and despair seep
through the battered earth.

Wealth gives a man power,
but steals his soul.

What more could I have done?
≋

A-4

With eight children
and a loving wife
to support,
I packed my salesman's trunk,
and traveled from town to town.

Mine was not an easy life—
countless hours
away from home,
endless train rides,
long laborious days
heaving under the weight
of wooden bowls
and boxes,
pastry rollers,
stirrers, scoops
and scrubbing sticks.
Long, lonely nights
spent in railroad sleepers
or seedy hotels,
guarding my trunkload
of woodenware.

Johnstown was different—
Mr. Quinn, the store owner,
so warm and friendly,
the hotel Hulbert House
so finely built,
so clean, modern and comfortable.

I was in the office
on the second floor
when an unusual
whistle sounded.
The hill is falling,
someone called—
The young teachers
screamed—
the walls caved in—
the ceiling dropped—
and the floor beneath us
washed away.

Such fine people, Nancy.
Such a fine establishment.
I couldn't wait to tell you.
I couldn't wait to come home.
≋

G-48, G-47, G-50

They found me
on the roof of my house,
a rope
twisted around my waist
and a child
curled in both my arms.

Hold on to the rope,
someone called.
Let go and save yourself!

How could I betray
the little ones
who clung
to my embrace?

My soothing words
were futile
against the flood,
but they comforted
the children,

without whom
there would be
no comfort ever.

≋

C-120

In truth, I never believed
the stories they told
about money
that grew on trees,
and streets
that were paved with gold.
But I did believe
in a chance to work hard,
to ease my hunger,
to send money home
and one day return
to the place of my youth.

I took an empty space
between the decks,
grateful,
even amid the stench
of waste, rotting food
and spew hardened
and hidden in the sawdust.

When the swaying stopped,
I spilled onto the shore,
full of reverent hope
and trembling dreams.

Strangers were not always kind
and the names they called me

I would not repeat,
but the fruit on my cart
was always fresh
and flavorful.
Business was good.
I married and had a family.
My children—
born in America—
were my pride

until the dam broke,
until the watery streets
overwhelmed us,

America was my pride.
≋

C-398

To live a life unknown
leaving nothing behind

but stripped bark
and whittled curls
a knot of wood
a few kind words.

To wander
where the whistle blows,

or follow
where the river flows,

and when it rises
to be lost,

and forgotten.

≋

JOE DIXON

Every day more people
are found or identified.
Every day small acts
of kindness awaken
our shattered courage.
But my own dreams,
once so buoyant and bright,
sink and drag
like mud-soaked stars—

my house in the mountains
with Maggie,
the blue sky above us
open and unstained,
my father beaming
with pride
when finally he understands
I didn't disobey, disregard
or defy—

I only dared dream
that life could be more
than soot and sweat.

It is all gone now.
All gone.

How is it vanished things
weigh so heavy?

≈≈≈

Kind people,
hearing of my mother,
crushed and crippled,

of my father,
trapped and drowned,

of my newsstand
lifted up
and washed away,

and the two younger
brothers
now left in my care,

raise money
to build and stock
a new stand for me.

Once again, I am
my own boss,
my own man—

such a hollow achievement
in a land emptied
of all dreams.

≋

Day by day
we slog
toward hope,
while a tired,
desperate
anguish
seeps through
the mud,
sludge
and weariness.

From hill to valley
distant voices echo—

the dam is weak,
the dam won't hold,

their self-serving folly
will destroy Johnstown—

words of warning
tossed
like pebbles in the sea,
wistfully retrieved
by those of us
who thirst for justice.

≋

One early evening,
Miss Barton,
the small woman in
the black dress
who has been written about
in all the papers,
approaches my newsstand.

Her steps are firm
but unhurried,
and before she speaks,
she studies me
with gentle eyes.

I've heard about you,
she finally says,
and have come to commend you—
you've embraced a difficult path
with courage and forbearance.

Miss Barton asks questions
about my father,
what he did before he died,
what he loved, how he lived.

He worked, I stammer, realizing
how little else I know—
he worked hard.
He loved his family.

I remember
Pa's disappointment
when I told him
about my newsstand.
He wanted me to work at the mill,
and I refused.

Miss Barton smiles.
Often in my work
on the battlefield,
I'd listen to the faltering
last words of young soldiers.
Many spoke regretfully
of love and gratitude
left unspoken.
They knew,
I'd whisper back to them.

She pats my hand.
Just as your father knew.

I nod and feel a sharp pain
like the splintering
of glass around my heart.

Miss Barton's eyes brim
with rugged tenderness—
You are young.
You have dreams—

I too have had faith
in something different,
something greater than the past.
Believe in yourself, Joe.
Believe in a better future
and be willing to fight for it.

I watch Miss Barton
walk away,
and wonder
at her words.

≋

The Chambersburg paper
advertises that a

complete, accurate
and well-illustrated history
of the Johnstown Flood
including
thrilling experiences,
pathetic incidents,
deeds of heroism,
unparalleled suffering,
devastation, death,
sympathy
and contributions

has already gone to press.

Who in Johnstown
would pay
one dollar and fifty cents
to remember
what we relive
whenever we
close our eyes?

≋

CLARA BARTON

In late afternoon,
when shadows
lengthen
and hearts begin
their melancholy
evensong,
I often call
on the young man
at the train station.

We are confidants,
Joe and I—
for he reminds me
of the young men
I met on the battlefield,
young men weary of war
and vanished dreams,
in need of gentle reminders
that beyond each suffering,
there is hope,
that to make one heart
stronger or less bitter
is to change the world.

Miss Barton! Joe says,
You've made the paper again!

He reads to me my own words:
"I've not met a man
from the governor down,
but is true to the trust
in his heart.
Put out of your hearts
all doubt and mistrust.
What you give will be
well done by."

It's true, I say.
Hearts are capable
of great generosity
and a giving heart
will not be disappointed.
To love despite
the wretchedness of war
or selfishness of man
is a noble calling.

My young friend
is not yet convinced,
but I see in his eyes
that he wants to be.

≋

JOE DIXON

The *New Era Lancaster*
and *Punxsutawney News*—
boldly proclaim

The Club Responsible
The Club to Blame

The *Johnstown Tribune*
agrees
the flood was not caused
by the vengeful
wrath of Providence,
but the selfish,
reckless, greed of Man.

Closer to the homes
of millionaire members,
the *Pittsburgh Dispatch*
prints a rejoinder.

Owners Say Stories
about the Dam's Weakness
Are Altogether False.

In hospital tents
and makeshift morgues,
amid the smell
of rotted wood and lime,

sorrow transforms
to bitterness.

Where will we find truth?
Where will we find justice?
≈≈≈

Finally, without comment,
even the Pittsburgh papers
print a list of club members.
I tear the list
from an unsold paper,
stuff it in my pocket
and memorize the names—

Andrew Carnegie
Henry Clay Frick
Andrew Mellon
Charles J. Clarke
Cyrus Elder
John Hay Reed
Philander Chase Knox
Colonel Elias Unger

and at least
three dozen more

men who lived lives
so bold and grand,
others sank into oblivion.

In my mind I write
what the papers
are afraid to say
and wonder if Maggie was right.
Maybe I should be a journalist.

≋

Andrew Carnegie
Henry Clay Frick
Andrew Mellon
Charles J. Clarke
Cyrus Elder
John Hay Reed
Philander Chase Knox
Colonel Elias Unger

All prosperous businessmen,
I think to myself,
who came to escape
the soot of Pittsburgh
and lingered in the haze
of their own cigars.

While I count, stack
and offer change,
phrases turn in my head.

Cocooned by wealth
and puffed with pride,
they celebrated
their own achievements—

smelting iron into steel
forging financial empires

congregating
in stately homes
and private clubs

wholly oblivious
to the struggles
of the hapless crowds
who toiled
in the city below them.

Your humble beginnings
inspired me, Mr. Carnegie,
but no amount of wealth
is worth another person's pain.

≈≈

Oklahomas arrive
to replace tents
and makeshift shelters.

Again, gratitude
is tempered
with disappointment
and frustration.

How will these flimsy,
ready-made houses
ever withstand
our Johnstown winters?

How will this small,
rickety shack
ever shelter me,
my mother,
Jacob and John?
≋

Daily, I scour the papers
for the slightest mention
of club members
or any scrap of news
about the South Fork
Fishing and Hunting Club.

I wonder if the members
even care.
Do they remember
how it feels to scrimp and save
and struggle—
to have but a single day a week
to spend with those they love?

His name was David,
I say to the dark.
He was born abroad
like you—
but not as lucky.
Her name was Maggie.
The willow ring I made for her
was worth so much more
than twenty thousand dollars.

I try to remember
Miss Barton's words,
but bitterness
chokes my heart.

≋

ANDREW CARNEGIE

The exposition was magnificent,
and at its entrance,
a proud monument for the ages—

more than eighteen thousand iron pieces
riveted and bonded one thousand feet
into the glorious Parisian sky—

a latticed testimony
to the power
of man's artistry
and engineering prowess!

How am I to be blamed
for the rushing water
of Johnstown
when my top hat
and heeled boots
were in Paris
celebrating man's
remarkable accomplishments?

Still, I mourned
the flooded factory town,

sending deepest sympathy
and abundant funds.

≋

CHARLES J. CLARKE

When word of the flood
was made known,
my South Fork friends
gathered
at my Pittsburgh home.

Mr. Reed and Mr. Knox,
members of the club
and our general counsel,
advised us to keep silent
about our association
with Lake Conemaugh.

Accordingly, we formed
the Pittsburgh Relief Committee,
collected money
to aid
in Johnstown's recovery

and vowed never to speak
of South Fork or the flood
ever again.

≋

HENRY CLAY FRICK

Advised to keep silent
about my connection
to the ill-fated
Lake Conemaugh,
I nonetheless expressed
my sympathy
with kind words
and a generous contribution.

Still, the working class
blames me for their troubles
and holds me in contempt.

It was not my fault!
One does not
become a millionaire
by coddling inadequacy—
I simply did not know.

There is also much
they don't know.

Look beyond marble stairs
and gilded frames.
For two long years,
I have watched

my own sweet child suffer
from an unknown ailment.

Wealth buys power
but it cannot buy peace.

≋

ANDREW MELLON

I began my business life
as a young child,
selling meadow grass
to farmers
five cents a bundle.

It is simply the way
of the world—
enterprising people
seize the moment.

How foolish of you
to demonize me
for the capriciousness
of nature
and incompetence
of man.

Still, I gave
one thousand dollars
to aid in your troubles.

Now wake up!
Make something
of yourself!
Seize the moment!

≋

CYRUS ELDER

From birth to death
we follow a trail
as if our own
hearts and hands
determined the route,
scorched the path
and scattered the seeds.

As the only resident
of Johnstown
to belong to South Fork's
elite club,
I sauntered
through the city
in my well-made suit
and white shirt.

Let anger be your armor,
but it will not be mine.
Sorrow moves
like dreamless ash on water.

Each of us is to blame.

We knew it in our hearts—
someday the dam would break.
≈≈≈

COLONEL ELIAS UNGER

It rained hard during
the night.
From my porch
at Lake View
it seemed the valley
had already
been swallowed
by water.

I dressed and hurried
onto the dam
to measure
the rising water.

Fearful of an overflow,
I ordered the Italian laborers
working on the sewage line
to dig another spillway
on the southeast side of the dam.

Surely, it is not my fault
that they hit rock
and failed in their assigned task.

Clearly, the Creator
intended to unleash his wrath
despite my most valiant efforts.
≋

JOE DIXON

I've begun to scour the paper
for other names too,
people I don't know—
people who have emerged
from briny shadows
to hold the club responsible—

Ann Jenkins,
visiting her family
here in Johnstown,

Nancy Little,
wife of a salesman
staying at the Hulbert House,
now a widow
with eight children—

both of them
plunged into despair,
both of them grappling
with a torrent of grief
and both of them

like me,

earnestly longing
for justice.
≋

ANN JENKINS

I will never recover
from the shock.
Had my foot
not been impaled
and pinned in place,
I too would have been
swallowed
by the brutal, rushing water.

Instead, I watched
in fear and horror
as my
mother,
father
and brother
were sucked into that dark,
tangled abyss.

Day and night
I see their faces.
Day and night
I hear their cries.

With seething, righteous anger,
my dear husband, James, insists
that those at fault
be held accountable.

Together we vow
that the self-absorbed,
self-serving members
of the South Fork
Fishing and Hunting Club
will hear my cries

and accept responsibility.
≈≈

NANCY LITTLE

I will try, John.
Though I tremble
like David before Goliath,
I will try to slay
the ruthless giant's heart.

Fifty thousand dollars
is just a number—
never meant to represent
your worth—
for how does one calculate
the value of a loving gaze,
or a father's steadfast
footsteps coming home?

My dear, dear husband!
Our spirits remain entwined
as they did when you
traveled from town to town,
your battered trunk
stuffed with woodenware,
your cheerful heart
overflowing with hope.
For the sake of our children,
I shelter that hope.

May the members
of the club hear me!
May they help support
our struggling family.

≋

JOE DIXON

In Eufaula, Alabama,
a cow was struck
and killed by a freight train.

The *Harrisburg Telegraph*
suggests farmers be kind
to toads
because toads
destroy thirty insects an hour.

The paper is filled with odd,
interesting tidbits
to share with my brothers.

But the trials
of Nancy Little
and Ann Jenkins?

Barely a mention.

One reads that news only
in the weary faces
of Johnstown.

≋

Yet incredibly,
even amid the lingering,
loathsome
smell of decay,
every dark night
awakens to a new day.

My ravaged town
reshapes
its battered limbs—
houses are built
stores are opened
banks are opened

and the heart of Johnstown—
the Cambria Iron Works—

slowly, faintly,
begins to beat again.

≋

GERTRUDE QUINN

We are going home!
Papa meets us
at the train station
on our return from Scottdale.
Now remember,
it's a much smaller house, he says.
He scoops me into his arms.
But finally we'll be together,
and in time,
we'll build a new house.

I bury my face in Papa's shoulder—
partly because I'm happy to see him
and partly because a strange
and terrible smell clings to the air.

We pass a large tree lying on its side
and Papa puts me down
but keeps hold of my hand.
We are almost there, he says.

A scrap of red-checked cloth
hangs from the topmost branch
of another fallen tree
and I think of the flag
Vincent saved for me.

I wish he were here
to wink and say,
Don't worry, Gertie,
in his cheerful voice.

We arrive at a small yellow house,
pale and pretty as a flower.
We're home, Papa says,
and Mama smiles.
It's perfect, James, she whispers
as he takes Marie from her arms.

See, Gertie! Helen says. *I told you
not everything is dark and bleak!*

I let go of Papa's hand
and, with my heart bursting,
race my sisters into our new home.
≋

JOE DIXON

Finally, I find
a small item buried
in the back pages
of a number
of papers,
including
the *Pittsburgh Press*
and *Washington Star.*

If the case by
Mrs. Jenkins is won,
the papers say,
there will be a regular
Johnstown flood
of litigation.

Is that why club members
remain silent?

≋

NANCY LITTLE

With its grand spire soaring
into the distant sky,
and its large arched stairways
looping throughout,
the new courthouse
is an imposing building—
the tallest in Pittsburgh.
I enter its foreboding doors
and feel myself shrink
into nothingness.
Then I remember—

you always left our house
with such high hopes
and cheerful words—
I won't be gone long!
Perhaps this time,
I'll sell enough
to stay home longer.

So with borrowed hope,
and mustered strength,
I climb the marble stairs
and breathe deep,
ready to aim
my tear-soaked stones
at the giant's
stone-cold heart.

≋

My solemn-faced attorney
pops up when he sees me.

I am so sorry, he says.
*The defendant's counsel
is in Europe
and the trial is postponed
until his return.*

Is there no end to injustice?
≈≈≈

ANN JENKINS

Counsel for the defense
is in Europe?

While we struggle
to find
a moment's peace,
the defense counsel
is on holiday?

Have they no sense
of decency?
No sense of guilt
or responsibility?

Defense travels abroad
while we stew
in sorrow and rage?

Have they no compassion?
Have they no humanity?
≋

NANCY LITTLE

Long months pass.
Again, I climb
the courthouse steps.

Again, cold archways
reach down
and envelop me
in an icy embrace.

My attorney waits
on a wooden bench,
head down,
hat in hand.

A scheduling conflict,
he says.
Another postponement.
I'm sorry.

Why are those
without fault
sorry
while the guilty
haven't a care?

≋

JOE DIXON

While the South Fork
Fishing and Hunting Club
remains anxious
to prove themselves
not culpable
in suits brought
against them
for the Johnstown
catastrophe,
a continuance
has been issued
by request
of the defense.

Just a small filler article—
hardly noticeable at all.

ANN JENKINS

Postponed.
Postponed.
Postponed.

How many times
can a trial
be postponed?

≋

NANCY LITTLE

Finally the cruel wait is over.
My attorney's briefcase is open,
his pages of facts and figures
spread neatly on the table.
I pray that the glistening
wood-paneled walls of justice
are stronger
than the battered, broken-down
walls of Johnstown.

My attorney stands
to address the jury.

Everyone here is aware
of the tragic events
of May 31, 1889, he says.
But I will repeat them.

On that terrible day,
twenty million tons of water
were unleashed
on the suffering community below.

More than two thousand people died.
Ninety-nine entire families.
Three hundred ninety-six children.

Large numbers often betray
the very facts,
the very individuals
they represent.

We understand a cup of water.
But a ton? Twenty million tons?
How can we comprehend this?

Today, I will bring
the immense tragedy
of the Johnstown Flood
into sharper focus.
But there is something else.
Something greater than the fate
of my client
and her eight children.

Many accounts
of the Johnstown Flood
would have us believe—
as I am sure defense
would have us believe—
that this tragedy
could not have been avoided.

After a night of heavy rain,
most accounts relate,
the South Fork Dam

simply succumbed
to the power of Nature.

THIS IS NOT TRUE.

Yes, it rained.
It rained hard.
But Nature
did not cause this tragedy.

Arrogance did.
Recklessness.
Power.
The selfishness
of a small group
of affluent men,

the very movers
and shakers
of our community
and country—
the elite members
of the South Fork
Fishing and Hunting Club—
are responsible
for the Johnstown Flood.

They were warned
about the rotting dam

and did nothing.
Let us not blame Nature
for the sins of man.

The words of my attorney
scorch my wavering courage.

My mouth turns dry.
My hands shake.

Who am I to challenge
men of money,
men of steel?

Men powerful enough
to move the century
into the future

without a single thought
of the wreckage
left behind?

≋

JOHN HAY REED

Before we begin,
let me first acknowledge
that the events
of May 31, 1889,
were indeed tragic.
Let me also offer its victims
my sincere condolences
as well as
the sincere condolences
of the generous members
of the South Fork
Fishing and Hunting Club
whom I represent today.
Many have contributed greatly
to the rebuilding of Johnstown.

The members of the South Fork
Fishing and Hunting Club
are bankers, entrepreneurs,
businessmen from all walks of life.
As the prosecution
has already pointed out,
they are the movers and shakers
of this great land.
None of them
is a common laborer—
and certainly none of them
is a dam builder!

This lawsuit and others like it
are ludicrous—

it was Providence
that unleashed the waters
of Lake Conemaugh,

Providence
that uprooted the trees,
crushed the houses
and allowed the flames
to spread at Stone Bridge.

To think otherwise
is simply absurd—
and I daresay
may also be an opportunity
to embarrass
and extort money
from the most affluent,
prestigious men of our time.

≋

NANCY LITTLE

I raise my quivering hand
and swear to tell the truth.

I order my voice to steady itself
and speak the words
I've carried in my heart
for months.

Is it Providence that failed
to replace the steel pipes
used to stem an overflow?

Is it Providence that inserted
the fish screens that clogged
the spillway with debris?

Is it Providence that lowered
the dam so two carriages
could conveniently cross at once?

And tell me,
is it Providence that deems
my eight children
should move through life
fatherless and penniless

while the rich
line their pockets
with gold?

≈≈≈

ANN JENKINS

At last my voice will be heard.
At last I am able to open
the floodgates of my heart
and let the whole world know
what I have endured.

Perpetual waves
swirl around me.
At night
pitiful wails awaken me.

Any recompense
will be but a drop
from your great ocean
of wealth—

It will not, I know,
stop the hauntings—

and yet,
their agony
my anguish

cry out for justice!
≋

PHILANDER CHASE KNOX

Clearly, we are all moved
by the personal recollections
of the suffering.
My co-counselor, Mr. Reed,
has already expressed
most eloquently
our deepest sympathy
in this dreadful,
unforeseen disaster.

But is there a single voice
able to prove
the personal negligence
of even one club member?

Of course not!

The members of the South Fork
Fishing and Hunting Club
are simply not liable
for the abiding, primordial,
inscrutable power of the divine.

Any fair-minded jury
must find in our favor.

Not a penny should be awarded
to the supplicants who sue!

≋

ANN JENKINS

Cowards!

Wealth is power
and those
with the most power
are deceived
by the dazzling gleam
of their gold,
impervious
to the trembling hearts
of we who suffer.

The spineless jury
had the chance
to hold the club
accountable.

But with averted eyes
and cold hearts,
they let themselves
be deluded
by distortions and lies.

The members
were not aware!

The members
are not responsible!

The flood was the will,
the power of Providence!

Chickenhearted yellow-bellies!
Weaklings! Toads!

≋

NANCY LITTLE

How can it be, John?

They flicked away
my pleading
like a draggled feather
on a morning suit.

How can it be
that all your hard work
is washed away,
all the struggles
we endured
for the sake
of the children?
How is it no one cares?

My beloved John!
I could fill
the emptied lake
with my tears.

≋

JOE DIXON

Whatever paper I read,
the headline is the same.

*The South Fork
Fishing and Hunting Club
Is Found Not Responsible
for the Johnstown Flood.*

Facts are facts
but sometimes
you need to dig deeper
to find the truth.

With every coin I collect,
I wonder
if selling papers
is as noble
as writing for them.

Every person has a story,
Maggie said.
But how many voices
are never heard?

How many stories
are buried because
to the rich and powerful
the truth is malleable?

A voice whispers
in my ear.
Honor them.
Tell their stories.

I whisper back,
I will.

≋

There was a time
Andrew Carnegie
was my hero.

There was a time
I measured success
in papers sold
and coins collected.

There was a time
I waited

for perfect moments
and perfect outcomes.

To love
despite the wretchedness of war
or selfishness of man
is a noble calling,
Miss Barton said.

There is a time
when each of us
must make our choice.

≋

GERTRUDE QUINN

Papa finds the brave man
who saved me
and shares some of
our relief money.
Money is just money, Papa says.
What Max gave us is
more precious than gold.

Papa is right.

The flood
washed away
my house
my tea set
my dolls and toys
but all I really miss
are the people—

Vincent, most of all.

We are lucky to have
a photograph of his kind,
handsome face,
but the photograph
does not show his smile
or how his eyes
twinkled when he spoke.

I miss Aunt Abbie too
and wish I had been kinder.
Aunt Abbie worried too much,
but always did
what she thought was right.
Mama says
that is all any of us can do.

I even miss the neighbors
whose names I don't remember,
the ones who visited Papa's store
and smiled at me
and patted me on the head.

Papa is right.
People are
more precious than gold.

School will be starting
later this year.
Papa says I must be brave
because some of my classmates—
and even my teacher—
will not return.

≋

Helen says we who survived
must be extra good
and always remember
what is important.
I am sure Aunt Abbie
smiled in heaven
when Helen said that.

Some grown-ups
bicker and brood,
but we children
have fun
scrabbling and scratching
the earth for treasure—

two- and three-cent pieces,
white pennies, half dimes—

I even found a shirt stud
with a sparkly diamond
and thought of Vincent
and all the sparkling treasures
I found in Papa's store.

Remembering Vincent
keeps him alive in my heart.
≋

On Papa's birthday,
I find Mama
in the tiny bedroom
she shares with Papa and Marie.
She is watching Marie sleep,
and I sit beside her on the bed.

I tell her about the party
we had planned
for her birthday.
It was going to be
a grand surprise.
Vincent said it was a great idea—
he was going to help me
find the sparkliest ribbon
to hang from the trees
and we were going to have
ice cream and cake and candy—

Mama puts her arms around me.
There will be parties again,
she whispers,
and ice cream,
and cake
and sparkly ribbon,
I promise.

I can tell Mama's
trying not to cry,

so we just sit,
rocking softly,
her arms around me
and mine around her.

Yes, Mama, I whisper,
there'll be parties again.
≋

CLARA BARTON

Medical needs have been
evaluated and addressed,
temporary shelters assembled,
donated food and clothing
efficiently distributed.

Summer has turned to fall
and my work here is done.
I shall treasure the kindness
and farewell gifts
bestowed on me,
but I need not a gold pen
or diamond locket
to remember
the brave and noble souls
whom I've met here—

Joe, the young man
selling papers
to support his family,

Max, who saved a little girl
by tossing her across the water,

the doctor with three cracked ribs
who delivered two babies
by the flickering light
of the Stone Bridge fire,

and so many more quiet,
unheralded heroes.

May Johnstown be ever blessed—

may she continue to rise
phoenixlike from the ashes,

a shining example
of humankind's
irrepressible spirit
and unblemished hope.
≋

JOE DIXON

Before she left, Miss Barton
stopped by my newsstand.
It heartens me to see you thrive,
she said.
Your father would be proud.
She told me her own father
had died many years before.
His patriot blood still runs
warm through my veins.
It was he who bade me
love mankind
and comfort the afflicted.
She smiled.
Even in death, those we love
are never far from us.

We say goodbye
and the heaviness
of that word
presses against my heart.

Those we love
are never far from us,
she repeats.

The cold October wind shifts,
and an almost forgotten afternoon
flutters into my mind.

≋

Maggie and I were walking
by the Stone Bridge
and a butterfly landed
on a nearby flower.

When my father was a child,
Maggie said,
a butterfly landed on his hand.
His mother had just died
and my father felt the butterfly
was trying to tell him something.
He thought about her all day.
Why had she landed on his hand?
What was she trying to say?

Did he ever figure it out?
I asked.

Maggie nodded.
The butterfly consoled him,
not just for the moment
she landed on his hand,
but for always,
even on the hard days
yet to come.
She reminded him
that once loved,
he would never be alone.

We watched our own butterfly
flit and flutter around us.

Maggie looked at me
with her big, bright,
beautiful eyes.

The day we buried my father,
a velvet-winged monarch
landed in the grass beside me.
I thought of my father—
and knew he loved me still.

How could I have forgotten
such a perfect day?

How many other moments
lie buried in my brain?

Such an ordinary day,
but it was perfect,
and even if I live forever,
this is the day
I want to remember.

≈≈

Bodies, many of whom
have never been identified,
continue to be brought
to Grandview,
our new cemetery.

Much work
remains
to be done,
but already,
there is talk
of building
a memorial
when enough
money
can be raised.

A monument perhaps,
or a row of white,
unmarked stones.

Something simple,
something peaceful,
something to balance
the chaos
of their last day.

≋

UNMARKED STONE

A caterpillar trudges
through fresh grass,
a solitary ant
crawls across
a nameless white stone.

It is quiet here.
Peaceful.

So many afternoons
I starved for this
and stayed away.

Now their nearness
comforts me.
≈≈≈

UNMARKED STONE

Billowing clouds
open to the sun
and bathe the world
in copper light,
a spider weaves
a shimmery web
in the branches
of the ancient pine.

High on the hill,
a tired-looking woman
clutches the arm
of a younger man.

A butterfly
with sapphire wings
flutters
between rows
and rows
of nameless stones.

Even bereft
of dazzling words,
beauty and love
endure.

≋

UNMARKED STONE

Sometimes people visit,
respectfully standing
on the hill,
praying, remembering,
wondering
what might have been.

Those of us
settled in the dust
hear them,
but remain quiet,
our time to worry or wonder
long passed into shadows.

Here in the cool earth,
it doesn't matter
if days were spent
in marble mansions
or wooden shacks

counting money
or sweeping floors

fishing in a sparkling lake
or catching frogs
by the Stone Bridge.

Here on the hill,
high above
springtime floods,

the blue sky
belongs to us all.

≋

JOE DIXON

The flood robbed us
of our family,
our friends, our dreams
for the future.
Sometimes, it seems
all that remains
is a somber field
littered with splinters
of the past—

water-stained photos

a chipped cup
from a child's
porcelain tea set

a wooden trunk
a silver bell

a waterlogged
composition book

keys, coins, buttons,
a torn flag
on a wooden stick
a pair of baby shoes.

Other times,
the sun lifts

the veil of grief
from our eyes—

a flower
pokes through the mud

a butterfly
quivers on the hillside.

On these days,
memories flow
lucid as dreams,

and hope returns
resilient as mountains.
≋

Eventually,
pathways
are cleared,
new houses
built,
new buildings
and businesses
established.

The sailboats
and man-made
lake
vanish
forever,
but silvery
pickerel,
bass and trout
once again
sparkle
in my sunlit
rivers
and find shelter
within and around
my sunken
logs and rocks.

Once again,
long,
drowsy days
meander
into weeks,
months,
years.

Yet even now,
when the mountains
weep,
when the rains
fall
swift and heavy,
my
scarred banks
overflow,
and from deep,
deep
within
my shimmering
water,
the spirits of
Johnstown
rise.

AUTHOR'S NOTE

The city of Johnstown is located on a floodplain at the junction of the Little Conemaugh and Stony Creek Rivers in Cambria County, Pennsylvania. In the middle of the nineteenth century, the South Fork Dam and Western Reservoir was constructed on the side of a mountain high above Johnstown. The dam was a massive earth-packed structure and the large artificial lake it created was intended to supply backwater for Pennsylvania's extensive canal system. When the railroad boldly roared into power, the canal became obsolete, and the South Fork Dam was left to deteriorate.

Eventually, a group of wealthy businessmen purchased the reservoir and surrounding land. The Western Reservoir was renamed Lake Conemaugh and the lush land that encircled it was transformed into a peaceful, private retreat. For nearly a decade, members of the South Fork Fishing and Hunting Club escaped the heat and noise of Pittsburgh by bringing their families to swim, fish and sail in the tranquil waters of Lake Conemaugh.

Though warned repeatedly that the dam that created the lake needed to be reinforced, the South Fork Fishing and Hunting Club did not take the precautions necessary to strengthen it. In addition, some improvements—made for the comfort and enjoyment of club members—actually weakened the dam. These improvements included lowering the dam so that two carriages could pass at once and inserting fish screens to keep expensive game fish from escaping.

On May 31, 1889, the South Fork Dam collapsed. Twenty million tons of water from Lake Conemaugh poured into Johnstown and neighboring communities. More than 2,200 people died, including 99 entire families and 396 children. Although some wished to categorize the Johnstown flood as a purely natural disaster, it was clear from the start that human negligence and hubris greatly contributed to this enormous tragedy.

The magnitude of loss from the Johnstown Flood is difficult to comprehend—homes and buildings were lifted from their foundations, trees ripped by their roots, train cars toppled and swept away. Some victims of the flood were not found until months later, and many were unrecognizable. More than 700 individuals were *never* identified and are buried beneath rows of white marble headstones in the Unknown Plot at Grandview Cemetery in Johnstown, Pennsylvania.

Flooded: Requiem for Johnstown is a work of historical fiction. The Johnstown Flood of May 31, 1889, was an actual occurrence, and characters noted by their full name truly existed. Experiences in the flood are based on written testimony and records of that fateful day. Gertrude Slattery Quinn wrote a particularly detailed memoir and I tried, for the most part, to keep the details of her amazing survival as she herself related them. However, the backstory, the relationships, conversations, motivations and monologues of each character, including Gertrude, are the work of my imagination.

In creating the characters noted by letter and number, I tried as best I could to cross-reference missing or unidentified victims of the Flood with recorded, poignantly brief morgue entries. *Male, 11 Years Old, Black Hair, Short Black Pants . . . Child about 5 Years . . . Unknown Female, 30 Years, Dark Luxurious Hair . . . Female, Burned beyond Recognition . . . Unknown . . . Unknown . . . Unknown . . .*

While much has been written about the Johnstown Flood, no one was ever held responsible for the failure of the dam, and it was difficult to find any detailed information about subsequent court proceedings. I have included whatever scant evidence I could unearth and for the sake of the story condensed the time line of these court proceedings. In actuality, the trials of Nancy Little and Ann Jenkins were not resolved until 1894, five years after the flood. Many believe that the lack of detailed information and numerous postponements reflected the power of the club members, which included some of the wealthiest and most influential men of the nineteenth century. It should be noted that while keeping silent about their membership, most though not all club members contributed to Johnstown's recovery. In addition to his initial monetary contribution, Andrew Carnegie rebuilt the town library, which today houses the Johnstown Flood Museum.

Whether truth, myth or creative vision, the mingling of the voices presented here reminds us that society's actions have consequences and that even the unnamed or long-forgotten lived lives worth remembering. I hope I have honored them all.

ACKNOWLEDGMENTS

The seeds for the this book were planted more than three years ago when my brother-in-law, Dr. Steven Burg, a history professor at Shippensburg University, invited me to his school to conduct a workshop on historical fiction. Pennsylvania has a prolific history and I set out to find an incident that would allow students to squeeze inside well-known facts to find the deeper truth—that link that connects the past to the present, that space where historical fiction finds its breath.

As the crow flies, Johnstown is less than eighty miles from Shippensburg and I thought its close proximity might be of particular interest to the students with whom I'd be working. I quickly discovered that location was the least important aspect of this story. While every catastrophe bears the mark of its particular setting, it is the human impact that matters most and that may be the most meaningful function of historical fiction.

I am forever grateful to Dr. Steven Burg for inviting me to Shippensburg. What began as a lesson plan became a journey of discovery.

I'm also grateful to Kaytlin Sumner, former curator of the Johnstown Area Heritage Association. Kaytlin graciously answered my earliest questions first through email and then when I visited the Johnstown Flood Museum. Gratitude also to Richard Burkett, president of JAHA. His thoughtful fact-checking and suggestions enriched my story. Thanks also to Andrew Lang, the present curator of JAHA for his additional interest and support.

Writing historical fiction means one's research is never really done. Did they even have those little flags on a stick in 1889? Thanks to Jeff Bridgman, a leader in the field of antique flags and textiles, I was happy to learn they did.

The look and feel of a book contributes to a reader's experience and I'm pleased and grateful that the masterful art director/designer Marijka Kostiw was again on my team.

I am also grateful for the detailed reading and sensitive comments of copy editor Joy Simpkins.

Thanks to the entire Scholastic Marketing, Publicity and Sales team and in particular Erin Berger, Lizette Serrano, Emily Heddleson, Rachel Feld, Lauren Donovan, Elisabeth Ferrari, Alan Smagler, Dan Moser, Elizabeth Whiting, Jody Stigliano and Jacqueline Rubin. I appreciate all you do to amplify one small voice.

A special thank-you to Benjamin Gartenberg, assistant editor, for his patience, thoroughness and dedication to this project.

As for my editor Tracy Mack—every writer needs someone like her in their corner. Because of Tracy, cement blocks burst into flowers.

In haunting line and color, Hadley Hooper captured the devastation and hope of Johnstown and I am grateful for her exquisite cover art.

I am also grateful for the support, kindness and advice of my agent Jodi Reamer.

Thank you Lesa Cline-Ransome for encouraging me to speak a little louder and for coaxing me out of my writing corner to mingle with a talented and supportive circle of writers.

Thanks also to Rosemary, Michael and Theresa for their unwavering belief in me and my stories.

Words written are words remembered and I would be remiss not mention the poets whose voices crept into this story: Sarah Doudney ("The Pure, the Bright, the Beautiful"), Henry S. Washburn ("The Vacant Chair"), Eliza Cook ("The Sailor's Grave"), Francis Miles Finch ("The Blue and the Gray"), and John Greenleaf Whittier ("Sunset on the Bear Camp"). Their works are all in the public domain but are gratefully acknowledged.

Finally, to Marc, Celia, Ben, Alex and S.B.—I wander many worlds, but you are mine.

In memory of my parents—

Helen Grace,

who instilled in me

a love for words,

and

Louis Thomas,

who often reminded me

that everyone has a story.

≋

Library of Congress Cataloging-in-Publication Data available

ISBN 978-1-338-54069-7

10 9 8 7 6 5 4 3 2 1   20 21 22 23 24

Printed in the U.S.A.   23
First edition, October 2020